20

SELECT PRAISE FOR

Hazy Fables Book #1

HOBGOBLIN

and the SEVEN STINKERS of RANCIDIA

★ Kirkus Reviews Best Books of 2019

★ Foreword INDIES Book of the Year Award Finalist

★ Kirkus Reviews Most Anticipated Middle-Grade Book

★ "Readers will giggle through every page
of this smart political satire."
—*Kirkus Reviews, starred review*

"Engages hard-to-please tween readers with
imaginative adventure, fun illustrations [and] silly fart
references...Read it together at bedtime to share laughter
and a positive message of empathy and inclusivity."
—*The Seattle Times*

"[A] hilarious second coming of *Snow White and the Seven
Dwarfs*...This story is like nothing you've ever read
before...You'll instantly fart with glee[.]"
—*Literary Features Syndicate*

To all the brave young humans fighting for their future.
– K.S.

ISBN: 978-1-948931-13-7

First edition: September 2020
Published by Hazy Dell Press, LLC

Printed in China.

10 9 8 7 6 5 4 3 2 1

Find all Hazy Dell Press books at hazydellpress.com.

ZOMBIE, OR NOT TO BE

Hazy Fables Book #2

BY KYLE SULLIVAN

ART BY DEREK SULLIVAN

HAZY DELL PRESS®
PORTLAND · SEATTLE

CAST of CHARACTERS

EDDA,
THE DEAD

NERIDA

BRAM

AUNT
AGONISTA

RICK

TABLE OF CONTENTS

THE ROTTEN STATE OF DEADMARK

Once upon a time, something was rotten in the state of Deadmark. But of course there was: Deadmark was filled with zombies, like me.

But we zombies didn't start there. Our story began in another country called Ignorway, just across the Undead Sea.

As far as zombie origin stories go, it was pretty standard stuff: The Ignorwegians didn't listen to their scientists, they destroyed their natural resources, they burned fossil fuels, and they polluted like there was no tomorrow.

One thing led to another until, *BAM!*—the climate went berserk, pollution and smog blocked out the moon and sun, the tides went completely out of whack, natural disasters became an everyday thing, and viruses spread like, well, viruses.

Luckily for me, one of those viruses was a zombie virus. It caused corpses to rise out of their graves and stalk through the streets on the hunt for brains.

And for a while, the zombies loved their living deaths in Ignorway. In the beginning, they indulged in a seemingly limitless supply of juicy brains while basking in a toxic and pleasantly spooky scenery that any zombie would love.

But the humans kept polluting, the chaotic weather worsened, and the disease-filled air got so bad that even zombies grew sick.

For zombies, it got scary in Ignorway—and not in a good way. They became concerned for their future. They began to think beyond their next meal.

On one hand, zombies existed because of climate change. While on the other hand, climate change put zombie existence in danger. What can I say? Death is complicated.

Either way, zombies knew Ignorway was no place to raise their next generation. So, just over one hundred years ago, they moved across the Undead Sea to create a new, rational, science-positive society. They named it Deadmark.

Believe it or not, zombies are not the slack-jawed, moaning goons from the human movies. We're usually very level-headed and reasonable. It's true we love brains, but more than that, we love *knowledge*. We love democracy, social harmony, literature, and dramatic arts. Above all else, we love the scientific method.

Deadmark's founding zombies built these values into the supreme document of the land: the ReConstitution. Among other things, the document forbids drilling for fossil fuels and requires a focus on renewable energy sources.

Although Deadmark was still affected by human-caused climate change, zombies now had the chance to make things better through science-based solutions. Their goal was to create an ideal society. Well, more ideal than Ignorway, at least.

To help guide the zombie society, the ReConstitution calls for an elected leader, known as the Lead Scientist, to work with a council of seven democratically elected zombies. Together, the Lead Scientist and the Elected Council make laws that follow the ReConstitution and, in theory, benefit all of Deadmark.

But even with noble ideals and a democratic system, zombies still needed to eat. To feed Deadmark, zombie brain hunters started sailing to Ignorway, harvesting delicious brains, and shipping them back by the boatload.

And despite our best attempts to harvest sustainably, humans didn't like being zombie food. Sometimes they fought back.

So, the founding zombies built a fortress on the north-facing shore to protect Deadmark from human attacks. They named it Zømborg Castle. Making it as uninviting as possible, they formed it from stone and human bones and constructed a colossal human skull, front and center.

Above the skull is a large clock erected to remind the Ignorwegians that their time would soon be up if they didn't stop destroying the environment.

Zømborg Castle is not only a major zombie landmark and historic site, it's also where I happened to grow up. The ReConstitution states that the Lead Scientist must live in Zømborg Castle, and for many years, my mom served as the Lead Scientist of Deadmark.

But here's where things really get weird: A few weeks ago, completely out of nowhere, my mom disappeared.

When I got the news, I was in class at my boarding school: Bittenberg University Prep in the country of Gormany. It was the second-to-last day of school before summer break. My Gormanic languages teacher, Miss Blutsauger, handed me a note. I read it, gasped, and jumped on the first train back to Deadmark. My death has been a mess ever since.

After arriving home in a panic, I learned that things were even worse than I had imagined. In my mom's absence, the Elected Council made the head-spinning decision to nominate my Aunt Agonista—the richest zombie in Deadmark—as their new Lead Scientist.

Admittedly, the ReConstitution doesn't provide a word of guidance for replacing a missing Lead Scientist. But still, the Elected Council's decision-making couldn't be worse. Up until her nomination, Agonista's only experience with the government was running a wide variety of businesses that had a habit of breaking Deadmark's environmental laws.

The Elected Council claimed it would be good to have the fresh perspective of a successful business-zombie to guide Deadmark, but I didn't buy it for one second. Not this business-zombie.

Agonista is the complete opposite of my mom. While most zombies still believe in Deadmark's founding ideals, some have staggered away from science. Some have moved toward a more destructive, money-driven, and Ignorwegian way of being. Agonista is one of those.

So, here I am, a twelve-year-old zombie student with a missing mom, a climate going haywire, and a new anti-science Lead Scientist in charge of Deadmark. These days, things in my world feel a bit topsy-turvy, to say the least.

Recent events have led me to question everything—family, zombiehood, science…the very nature of existence. My mind is all mixed up and frantic. And without my mom, I'm not sure what to do or who to turn to. Being a zombie kid is hard enough as it is, but this is all too much.

My name is Edda. This is my story. It's the story of a zombie with a lot on her brain.

CHAPTER ONE

CHAPTER ONE
A SEA OF TROUBLES

"Who's there?" squeaked the vampire bat. "Is that Edda?"

The wind screamed through my tangly white hair as I clung to the turbine's ladder. I was about twenty feet above Zømborg Castle's northern wall with the castle's towers and ramparts stretching out beneath me. It was bitterly cold, even for a zombie.

I carefully set my socket wrench down beside the turbine's turned-off motor. With one arm crooked through the ladder, I used my free hand to shield my bloodshot eyes from the wind as I squinted into the dark, angry sky.

"Yes, Bram—it's me!" I called out in a loud whisper.

Despite the screeching gusts and the wind turbines whooshing furiously along the castle wall, I could hear my friend's frantic squeaking. But he was nowhere to be seen.

Gray, ashy flakes swirled around me, clouding my vision. It was pollution blowing in from Ignorway's factories across the Undead Sea.

It was as if the skies themselves were flaking apart. Kind of like my reality.

Suddenly, Bram rode in on a gust of wind and popped up right in front of my face.

"Hey, Edda!" he squeaked, flapping wildly. "I assumed it was you, but you know how terrible I am with the whole echolocation thing. I'll just meet you down on the rampart."

The strong winds would have made things difficult enough, but the smartphone Bram clutched in his little bat feet made it almost impossible for him to fly at all.

"I'll be right down," I whispered as loud as I dared so that Bram could hear me over the wind, but not so loud that I could be heard by the zombies partying in the courtyard below the castle wall.

After tightening one last bolt, I carefully replaced the turbine's casing. I returned my socket wrench to my tool belt and wiped my hands one at a time on the sleeves of my worn-out black-and-gray flannel.

Lately, I had taken to wearing black clothes to mourn my missing mom and to protest the Elected Council's decision to make my Aunt Agonista the Lead Scientist. After my mom disappeared, they barely searched for her at all before replacing her with my aunt. It all seems a little too hasty, if you ask me.

With a sigh, I switched the turbine on. Immediately, the blades began spinning violently in the gale-force winds, causing the entire turbine tower to wobble. It felt good to accomplish something, however small, even though it probably made no difference.

And really, *can* I make a difference? I've been racking my brain for an answer. Do my actions matter at all, or is everything on a fixed crash course that's out of my control?

Before things got scrambled up, I didn't really ask questions like this. I always had two pillars to rely on when troubles arose: my mom and science. Now my mom was gone and there was nothing science could do to make her reappear.

With these thoughts clanging around in my head, and with slow and cautious steps, I made my way down the ladder to the castle wall below.

After a few rungs, a particularly powerful blast of wind stopped me cold. As I held on tight and waited for the wind to change direction, I looked out to the north, over the toxic, churning waves of the Undead Sea.

Green vapors wisped off the black water as jagged, white-capped spikes rose and fell. Powerful swells gathered and slammed into the castle wall made of gray stone and human bones. Some of the waves had enough momentum to splash up and onto the rampart wall a good forty feet above sea level. It felt like the waves were trying to break through and wash my whole world out to sea.

The powerful gust moved on, and after a deep breath, so did I.

The turbine I clung to was just west of the enormous Ignorway-facing skull and clock at the front of Zømborg Castle. I could hear the pendulums swinging inside each of the skull's cavernous eyes. With perfectly timed clanks, they marked the seconds that were tick-tick-ticking away.

Beyond its symbolism, the castle's clock was also useful. Only moments ago, its glum chimes let me know it was a quarter to noon. Without the pollution-blocked moon and sun to guide us, clocks were the only way to track the time.

As I made my way down, I could hear trumpet blasts, drumbeats, hoots, whoops, and hollers coming from the courtyard below the castle wall. Most zombies were curled up in their graves at this time of day, but by the sounds of it, this party was not slowing down—or shutting up—anytime soon.

I looked down in fury at the gleeful Elected Council. They

were celebrating their decision to make Agonista the Lead Scientist by guzzling glasses of bubbly brain fluid and nibbling fancy brain appetizers on little toothpicks.

As if absolutely nothing was wrong, they munched cheerfully away on intestine-wrapped brainstem bites, lobe loaf, cerebellum tartlets, and pickled brain clusters.

A disturbing thought crossed my mind as I watched these misguided zombies and their brain banquet: Were they eating leftovers originally intended for my mom's unsuccessful search party?

My thought was interrupted by Agonista's witchy cackle rising up with the wind from the courtyard. With a primal growl, I stopped on the ladder to glare at her. Tall and lanky as a skeleton, she was talking with a council member and flailing her wispy limbs to make her point.

You might think someone as rich as Agonista would have a sophisticated sense of style. But you'd be wrong. Instead,

she wore a black turtleneck and round sunglasses, despite the lack of sunlight. Jutting out to the side of her puffy white hairdo was a large, metallic (very tacky) wireless earpiece for her smartphone.

It was surreal to think of this zombie in charge of Deadmark. While owning businesses isn't a bad a thing on its own, Agonista has always skirted the rules and environmental laws established for the greater good. Her ambition and greed made her the richest zombie in Deadmark, but at what cost to the rest of us?

I couldn't prove that she had evil intentions as Lead Scientist, but my hunch was big enough to qualify me as a mad scientist's assistant.

Looming at Agonista's side were Deadmark's fiercest brain hunters, Squeak and Gibber. Apparently, Agonista had drafted them into some kind of security role. Squeak was very small and rode in a harness that Gibber, a remarkably tall and lumbering zombie, wore on his back.

They wore spiky armor and grungy black camouflage to help them blend in with Ignorway's polluted environment when they were on the hunt. An arsenal of brain-hunting tools hung from a strap across Gibber's chest, including hammers, hooks, bone saws, and ice cream scoops.

Their eyes darted around as if on the lookout for intruders. Luckily, they didn't think to look up.

Resuming my descent down the ladder, I kept my eyes on the grotesque scene below. There I was, stuck between raging waters and a money-grubbing aunt.

"A sea of troubles on both sides," I muttered to myself.

I hopped down from the ladder onto the castle wall, which was a few dozen feet above the courtyard party.

Small energy-efficient lights cast a silvery glow among the drifting pollution flakes. The stone wall was peppered with human skulls, femurs, and other bones. A zombie's idea of a classy architectural touch.

Bram was there waiting for me, leaning nervously against the stone-and-bone wall.

He was back in his vampire form, with a shock of thick black hair crowning a dark green face. Along with a hoodie, he wore a backpack and puffy pants featuring a pattern of neon-colored bats.

And, as always, he wore a pair of fun, colorful sneakers.

Bram's sneaker collection was an object of fascination for me, because zombies don't wear shoes at all. Zombie feet require a certain amount of ventilation that shoes and socks just don't allow.

"It's 11:53," Bram said. He held his phone away from his body as if it were a wooden stake. "That means this thing, this illusion—whatever it is—will call in seven minutes."

Bram and I were here because of a phone call. Well, a video call. Someone—something—had been waking Bram up with a video call at noon sharp for the past two days. Just as he got a glimpse of a creature, the call would cut out. And the weirdest part: He said the thing resembled a strange version of my mom.

"Hopefully your reception is better up here than in the Glob Theater," I said.

The Glob Theater is where we've been crashing. When I returned from Gormany, I discovered that Agonista had taken over not only my mom's graveroom in the castle's northeast sector, but mine as well.

I found my things jumbled inside a crate at the bottom of the steps that led up to my old room. Agonista didn't even give me a reason for kicking me out of the castle. But, as Lead Scientist, I guess she didn't have to.

With my school on summer break, and my graveroom stolen from me, I had nowhere to stay. So, I've been sleeping in the Glob's wardrobe room where my friend Rick runs the show. Bram has been sleeping in the Glob's attic.

"At least up here we'll be able to see if anyone creeps up on us," I said, glancing in both directions along the empty castle wall. It could be paranoia, but I had the uneasy feeling that Agonista was watching me lately. That's why Bram and I avoided detection by taking separate routes.

"This is really weird and scary, but it's kind of fun, right?" Bram asked as he propped his phone on the rampart ledge between us. He forced out an unconvincing chuckle, his fangs glinting faintly in the lights. "I mean, how often do you get a phantom phone call?"

Even though I wouldn't characterize this as "fun," exactly, it felt a lot better with Bram around. He's such a calm, stable friend. He could be spending his summer break anywhere—Gormany, Franke, Fangland—but he decided to stay here to hang with me.

I met Bram on the first day of class at Bittenberg University Prep. We became instant friends. Bram grew up in Gormany, a country of mostly vampires, so he showed me the ropes and helped me adapt to the vampires' social and cultural way of death.

In Gormany, Bram would never be outside at this time of day, since sunlight turns vampires into stone. In Deadmark,

however, he was safe from the sun because the pollution billowing in from Ignorway completely blocked it out.

"What were you doing up there, anyway?" Bram asked, pointing up to the turbine.

"The tool belt was supposed to be an excuse for me being up here," I explained. "If anyone asked, I was going to tell them I was fixing a wind turbine. Then, when I got here, one of the turbines was actually broken, so I fixed it."

We both looked up at the rapidly spinning blades. "Zømborg Castle's renewable energy technology has been falling apart lately," I said. "First the hydroelectric generator, then the bone compost biofuel converter, and now a wind turbine."

Glaring down at Agonista, I wished I could shoot fireballs out of my eyes. "I can't help but blame her," I said.

Agonista was telling a story to a few of the Elected Council zombies. She wore a smile that nearly cracked her face in two.

"She smiles and smiles," I sneered. "But I know she is a villain."

"Edda, you're gnashing your teeth," said Bram, his face beaming sympathy.

Bram and I waited as pollution flakes swirled around our heads, poisoned waves crashed into the castle wall, and the party banged and clattered below.

"I really hope this isn't some silly daymare brought on by

the scary slayer movies I sometimes watch," Bram said. "Even when I see it, I can't believe it. The calls are so choppy, and my screen is really cracked. But it does look a little like your mom. Once, I even thought I heard it say your name…but the reception cut out before I could ask it questions."

I don't actually own a phone, so if this thing is trying to reach me, it has no way to call me directly. I have pretty strong feelings about so-called "smart" phones. I've seen zombies walking around the streets of Deadmark, mouths agape, staring at their devices like mindless humans. Not my style.

Bram put his hand on my shoulder. "Edda, you're gnashing again."

"Oh, sorry," I said. The way things were headed, I was going to grind my teeth into dust by the end of the week.

"So, it's 11:58," said Bram. Trembling slightly, he grabbed his phone and held it closer so we both could see the screen. "Are you ready for this?"

"Yes," I said. I reached out my hand to help him steady the phone. "I'm ready."

Eyes and mouths open wide, we stared at the phone's cracked screen. Bram had dropped it countless times, both as a vampire and as a bat.

Breathless, we watched the phone's digital clock flip to 11:59. For the next sixty seconds, we didn't dare blink.

The wind howled around us. At the precise moment Bram's phone showed 12:00, Zømborg Castle's clock boomed across the furious sea.

BONG!...BONG!...BONG!...BONG!...BONG!...BONG!... BONG!...BONG!...BONG!...BONG!...BONG!...BONG!

Then, at once, before the twelfth tone had faded away, we both recoiled in fear when a death metal guitar riff blared from the phone. It was Bram's ringtone. He hastily silenced it as the words *UNKNOWN NUMBER* crawled across the screen.

Bram looked at me, fanged mouth open in awe. I took a breath and nodded.

With an unsteady finger, he touched his screen to answer the call. An image struggled to materialize behind the cracked surface.

The video connection popped and fizzled. What we saw came through weak and glitchy, but what we saw was unmistakable.

My mind burst with horror.

It looked like my mom. And it looked human.

CHAPTER TWO

ENTER HUMAN

"**D**o you see it, too? Am I hallucinating?!" cried Bram.

"We should let it speak!" I whispered, trying to keep it together.

The phone's wavering light cast an eerie glimmer as we huddled down behind the wall's ledge.

Wherever the figure was calling from, it was very dark, with dull flickering light, as if lit by torches or dim bulbs. It was surrounded by what appeared to be grimy rock.

Despite the darkness, the bad connection, and the fractured screen, I could make out something resembling my mom wearing a hardhat with a turned-off headlamp. The thing had dirt smudges across its face, and its mouth was moving, but the connection only allowed gasping, guttural noises to come through.

"If you have a voice, speak to me!" I loud-whispered. There was no way this could be my mom. I refused to believe it. "What are you? A human? A goblin? A ghost? Why are you scaring us like this?"

"Bah— Gah— Ed— Da—" was all that came through the staticky line.

"Speak! Speak! You have to speak!" I said, louder than before.

This was all so incredibly strange. This thing sort of looked like my mom, but its nose was fleshy and filled out like a human's, and it had lush and curly black hair instead of the white, matted, knotty hair that I remembered. Most striking of all were the sparkly white eyes with bright green irises staring back at me.

If this was a disguise, we were dealing with a professional.

A gust of wind screamed past. Bram and I leaned in closer to the phone to hear what the figure was saying.

"Edda, my dear," said the humanlike form, its voice finally breaking through. Despite sounding frantic, the voice was smooth and even—not the scratchy voice of a zombie. "I'm so glad I finally reached you. Reception is very spotty in this coal mine."

It looked over its shoulder and paused as if waiting for someone to pass, and then: "Listen, I don't have much time. We're not allowed to use phones at work, but one of my coworkers sneaks one in and lets me use it at lunchtime."

"Who are you, and why are you calling Bram's phone from a coal mine?" I demanded. I looked at Bram and saw a face filled with fear and wonder.

"Listen, Edda," it said. "I know you're finding this hard to believe. But I'm your mother. I'm a human now."

My body buzzed with terror. Was I losing my grip on reality? Had I already lost it?

"I'm doomed to walk among the humans in Ignorway, toiling in this old coal mine on the search for fossil fuels." It pointed its phone's camera down a dark cavern of rock and then returned its face to the screen.

"But don't feel sorry for me," it said. "I would tell you more about what it's like here, but it would give you daymares for months. It's horrific."

"Try me," I said, eyes narrowing in determination. What could be worse than a weird human thing pretending to be my mom?

"Choke Industries has completely taken over," it said. "They're the wickedest corporation in Ignorway. They own countless factories and mines, including this one." The figure

turned its head and pointed to the logo displayed on the side of its helmet. It was a puffy cloud of pollution with a dollar sign in the middle. Beneath the logo were the words "*Choke Industries, Inc.*"

"The streets are drowning in trash, and the sky is made of smog," it said. "Choke's factories, mines, and quarries have poisoned the air, land, and water. As you know, unchecked pollution killed off animals and trees long ago. Now, even Ignorwegian crops have been wiped out. The only food left is gross artificial stuff made by Choke, like this plasticky mush they're constantly guzzling."

The thing held up a bucket-sized plastic cup with a straw at the top. The container also bore Choke's logo.

"Disgusting," I said. This was a very detailed account told with convincing distress. It even had props. Could it be a talented performer trying to scam me?

"It is horrid, but that's not why I called," it said. "Deadmark is in danger, Edda. I'm afraid my humanization might be part of a much larger plan."

"Wait—you're saying someone humanized you?" I asked. "That's a very serious accusation."

"Yes," it said, bristling. "A humanization most foul. Not to mention strange and unnatural."

"Tell me what happened!" A series of possibilities flashed

through my mind, but I needed to hear it from the source.

"A snake, Edda," the figure hissed. "A slithering, double-crossing snake slipped something into my glass of brain fluid. I'm not sure what it was, but it moved through my body in an instant, smoothing my scaly zombie skin, uncurdling my blood. Before I knew what was happening...I was human."

An icy shiver slinked up my spine and through the tips of my hair.

"After she humanized me," it said, "the same snake deceived and bribed the Elected Council into naming her the Lead Scientist of Deadmark."

"Aunt Agonista!" I yelled, clenching my fist. I was so mad that I didn't care if the courtyard party heard me.

"Yes," it said, eyes cast downward in grief. "Sadly, I've never trusted my sister. She was always driven by greed and profit. She never cared about the environment or the community. But I could never have guessed the depth of her wickedness."

KA-POW! There was an explosion in the coal mine. The video feed shook violently for a few seconds. When the face returned to our screen, dust drifted down around it, followed by small falling chunks of rubble that clicked off its hardhat.

Bram and I could hear voices and shouting in the background. The figure looked over its shoulder, and when the voices dwindled, it continued.

"They've run out of coal. They're using dynamite to find new deposits," it said. "They haven't found anything yet besides useless multicolored rocks. But I don't have much time—my boss will be back any second."

KA-POW! Another explosion rocked the mine. The thing ducked its head and stared wildly into its phone. "Listen carefully, Edda: I'm concerned that Agonista doesn't believe in anything except her own greed. I'm worried that she's going to run Deadmark like she runs her businesses—by ignoring climate science to make money, no matter the consequences."

"What a piece of work she is. I can't believe she's in charge of Deadmark!" I pounded my fist on the stone wall. Although this thing may be faking, its words about Agonista seemed to align with my hunch.

"Yes, Edda," it said. "The Elected Council has been lied to and bribed. I'm afraid Agonista is going to amplify the growing anti-science movement that's taken hold. We can't let her transform Deadmark into another Ignorway by turning zombies away from science."

I moved my head around to look at this thing from different angles. It was chilling. From one angle, it was a hideous imposter, nothing like my mom. But from another angle, I could see my mom's pleading eyes staring back at me. Was I just getting caught up in the moment?

"Listen, I'm sorry," it said, "but my lunch break is almost over—"

"Please," I begged. "Before I can fully believe your story, I'm going to need more information."

"As quickly as I can, here you go," she said with a hasty breath. "Once I was humanized, Agonista sent Squeak and Gibber after me to eat my brain. I was able to outrun them and jump into a small fishing boat tied to the docks at East Ganglia Bay. I paddled out into the Undead Sea and eventually met up with a ship filled with zombie-hunting humans. They took me to Causewoe, the capital of Ignorway, and I was promptly shuttled off to this coal mine."

"Hey, you!" said a husky voice offscreen. Bram and I both jolted at the unexpected interruption. "No phones allowed!" The phone screen became a blur, and there were sounds of a struggle.

"It's all so very horrible! Oh, so horrible!" shrieked the figure. The screen was chaotic with movement that we couldn't make out. "Please do not stand for it, Edda! Don't let Agonista's anti-science nonsense lead the Elected Council astray. Don't let Deadmark turn into Ignorway!"

We could hear grunting and yelling, and then the face of the figure-who-was-possibly-my-humanized-mom filled the screen again.

"Whatever you do, do not turn your back on science!" it yelled. "Have faith in Deadmark. Trust your friends. Don't forget about me!"

I wanted so badly to believe it was her. To know it was her without a doubt. I wanted to call out, "I'll never forget you, Mom! I love you!" But it was too late.

The call had ended.

CHAPTER THREE

A MIND IMPATIENT

I was shocked to the core of my zombiehood. My mind throbbed with fear and confusion. I sat there staring blankly at one of the human skulls peering out from within the rampart wall.

Could this really be happening? I gagged at the thought of my mom living a human life in Ignorway. I seethed at the greed of my evil aunt. I felt the weight of unimaginable responsibility pulling me back into the ground.

"Is it true, Bram?" I asked. "Is my mom a human? Is Deadmark really on the brink of ruin?"

"I…I don't know," said Bram, as he slipped his phone back into his pocket. "It could be a high-tech fake. These days, there are a lot of filters and special effects that can make bogus videos seem very real."

I stood up, pulled at my hair with both hands, and groaned in dismay. "This is so unfair! One minute I'm minding my business in Gormanic languages class, and then *WHAM!*—out of nowhere my mom disappears, all of Deadmark is hanging in the balance, and somehow it's up to me to fix it."

Bram stood up beside me, his face displaying a combination of pity and fear. Realizing I was still clinging to two knotty handfuls of hair, I quickly pulled my hands down and put them in my pockets.

"Am I losing my grip on reality, Bram?" I looked directly into his eyes for reassurance.

He didn't answer right away. "No, Edda," he finally said. "You're just going through a lot right now."

My eyes narrowed. Was he just being nice? "If I did lose my grip, would you tell me?" I asked.

"Yes, Edda, of course," he said, seeming a little offended. "I can't say I know exactly how you feel, but it's normal to feel upside down when something bad happens. When my Great-Aunt Lilith was turned to stone a few years ago, it felt like death as I knew it would never be the same."

"I hear you, Bram," I said with a sigh.

Around us, pollution flakes whirled, the wind wailed, party

noises clamored on, and waves pounded incessantly.

Yellow lights dipped and swayed on the horizon. From this distance, I couldn't tell if they belonged to zombie brain-hunting ships or human zombie-hunting ships.

"This is all so strange and troubling," said Bram.

"It's wild," I said, "but if that thing is telling the truth, doesn't everything kind of make sense? Because of my aunt's evil deeds, the whole world has flipped on its head: My mom is a human, zombies care less and less about science, and an anti-science bully is in charge of Deadmark."

"I don't know," said Bram, his hand on his forehead. "None of it makes sense to me. For one thing, how could Agonista have turned a zombie into a human by putting something in a drink? Does such a thing even exist?"

"Actually, yes," I said, my eyes on the crashing waves. "I don't know where Agonista got hers, but before I left for Gormany, my former lab partner and I accidentally created a terrible substance that we called 'humanizer mutagen.'"

Bram looked at me as if I had garlic stuck in my teeth. "Um, Edda, what are you talking about?"

"Her name's Nerida," I said, my eyes still on the water. "Back when she and I were lab partners, we were committed to finding a way to reintroduce life into Deadmark's bleak ecosystem. Plants were extinct because the sun was blocked, but we thought we could make a plant that exists on what zombies exist on…brains."

Bram scratched his head. He was clearly struggling to process this information.

"We were successful—we were able to create a brain-eating plant, and some animals as well—but there was a lot of trial and error along the way. Sometimes the results of our experiments were expected, and sometimes they were shocking. By far, the most surprising thing we discovered was a formula that appeared to transform zombie cells into human cells."

"Humanizer mutagen," whispered Bram.

"Yes, exactly," I continued, "but we didn't know what to do with it. While it was clearly a very destructive substance, we thought it might lead to more discoveries down the road. But…" I cast my eyes downward. "Our friendship fizzled out and we stopped talking. I'm not sure what she ever did with it."

Bram frowned as he rubbed the back of his neck. "So, um," he began, searching for words. "Is it possible that Nerida gave Agonista the humanizer mutagen?"

"No!" I exclaimed, surprising myself. "No, Nerida would never do that. We may not be close anymore, but I know she would never join forces with Agonista."

I sighed. The situation still gave me a sinking feeling in my stomach, so I tried not to think about it too much. "I'm sure she got rid of it," I said. "But it's not like I could just walk into her lab and ask her about it. She's never forgiven me for enrolling at Bittenberg Prep and moving to Gormany. She thinks I abandoned her and all of the scientific progress we made together."

The emotions started gushing out from the deep, murky place I had tried to bury them. "But, really, my decision was never personal," I said, raising my voice. "Her scientific focus is botany—marine botany—and I couldn't spend my whole death studying water plants. I mean, the world is disintegrating around us, and she's fixated on seaweed!"

I had worked up so much steam, I was yelling by the end of my rant.

"Yikes, Edda, it's fine." Bram held up his hands defensively. "I shouldn't have brought it up."

Between the death-altering phone call and the old arguments with Nerida playing out in my head, I felt like I was losing it. And the concerned look Bram was giving me certainly didn't help. I know he was just being a good friend, but after that phone call, I was going to need more than just sympathy.

I pulled out a magnifying glass from my tool belt. "Bram, please swear on this magnifying glass that if I start to act irrationally, or if I seem in any way disconnected from reality, you'll tell me."

I held the magnifying glass toward him. We were both committed science students. I knew he would take a magnifying glass oath very seriously.

"I promise," he said, his hand on the instrument. "If I see something, I'll say something."

"OK," I said, with an exhalation of breath. "Thanks, Bram. I appreciate it."

We stood there without a word. Bram continued to side-eye me uneasily as I stared across the frenzied sea.

Several hours later, we were seated at a booth in our favorite diner, the Brain Fry. It wasn't until the late-day crowd began shuffling in that I realized we had been sitting there all afternoon.

The Brain Fry featured a black-and-white color scheme, with vibrant splatters of red paint splashed across the walls, floor, booths, and tables. There was nothing like a little splatter décor to stoke the appetites of late-day zombie diners.

Some shuffled in wearing shabby lab coats, looking tired from day shifts in the lab. Others appeared to be hungry college students pulling all-dayers, cramming for final exams.

Although there was an emerging anti-science trend in zombie society, it was nice to see that some zombies were still focused on our founding principles of science and knowledge.

Science-focused or not, many customers and Brain Fry staff recognized me as the daughter of the missing Lead Scientist. I tried my best to ignore their gawking stares and pitying looks.

I was slurping on my third occipital shake out of a metal cup as I jotted down half-thoughts and diagrams in my science journal. My thoughts were scattered, more tangled than my hair. Writing and doodling helped organize my thinking and put things into perspective. Or so I hoped.

Bram was slumped dead-asleep across from me, an empty bowl that once contained a heaping serving of blood pudding in front of him. Beside the bowl was an open book that he had fallen asleep reading: a mind-control manual called *Invite Yourself In*. A small trickle of red-stained drool ran from his open mouth and down his chin.

While Bram slept, my mind was whizzing faster than the wind turbines above the castle. I needed to determine if the thing in the coal mine was actually my mom and not some sort of elaborate hoax. But I needed more evidence.

The white pages in my journal were filling up with my feverish scribbles, none of it making sense. *Words, words, words,* I thought to myself.

Unable to organize my thoughts into sentences, I started doodling a menacing portrait of Agonista. I chuckled as I sketched a comically large wireless earpiece, bigger than her head.

Typically, I would go the scientific route to solve my problems. But these weren't typical times. The figure in the coal mine urged me to trust in science, but if that thing was truly my humanized mom, then science didn't help her very much, now did it?

I let my mind wander as I made Agonista's hair fluffier and fluffier. *Maybe in this instance,* I thought, *science isn't the answer. Maybe these unpredictable circumstances require something a little more unexpected, a little more chaotic.*

Then, like an energy-efficient lightbulb switching on, an idea illuminated my dark mind. I lifted my head from my journal.

"That's it!" I shouted, stabbing my pen in the air like a sword.

Bram jumped out of his death-slumber, and several zombie students turned to look at me in surprise. They whispered to each other as if I wouldn't notice, as if I hadn't noticed them

glancing at me like I was some kind of tragic antihero since they staggered in.

"What—Who?!" Bram struggled up from his sleeping position and wiped the drool from his chin.

"Agonista is never going to reveal anything if she's suspicious of me," I said. I kept my voice low and watched as the zombie heads around us returned to their appetizers of stem fries, temporal tempura, and the Brain Fry's specialty—a hippocampus hummus that the menu promotes as "unforgettable."

"I need to remove her suspicion," I continued. "Make her believe I'm not a threat."

"Sorry, but I don't get it," said Bram, still blinking the sleep from his eyes.

"I need to act like I don't suspect a thing," I said. "Like I'm sympathetic to her perspective. Like I'm so upset that I'm not thinking clearly."

Bram's confused expression didn't change.

"Don't you see, Bram? That way, Agonista will let her guard down, and we can get close enough to her and the Elected Council to get the information we need to take action. To know for sure that thing in the coal mine is telling the truth."

The plan whirred through my turbulent mind. "If Agonista thinks I'm broken, distraught, and on her side," I said, verbalizing my thoughts as they arrived, "she'll never know how dangerous I really am."

Then it hit me. I knew exactly how to act like I was receptive to Agonista's anti-science ways. To act like I wasn't myself, like I had completely changed from who I used to be.

I had to act like a human.

Frantically, I jumped out of the booth, knocking into the table and sending my empty shake cups clinking sharply across the floor.

"Wait!" called Bram as he clambered up from the booth and snagged his book. "Where are you going?"

"Where all actors go, Bram. To the Glob Theater!"

CHAPTER FOUR

THROWING ABOUT
OF BRAINS

The zombies of Deadmark had risen from their graves to greet the night. Bram and I made our way through Cerebrum Street's bustling evening crowd as we discussed my still-developing plan.

Pollution flakes and fog billowed and swirled beneath energy-efficient streetlamps. Many of the bulbs were broken— too many to feel like an accident. The remaining bulbs struggled to illuminate the cobblebone road.

"I don't know if the coal mine caller is telling the truth," I said, jamming my hands into the pockets of my tattered jeans, "but I would not be shocked if Agonista is trying to hide some

41

very bad deeds—hidden secrets that we need to bring to the surface."

"Well it's a good thing zombies are experts at bringing buried things to the surface," said Bram, snickering at his own joke.

We made our way past the homes and buildings of Cerebrum Street, all made of stones and bones and shaped like skulls in the traditional zombie style. Most were tricked out with renewable energy gizmos and scientific equipment like wind turbines, barometers, and satellites.

I tried my best to avoid eye contact, but the passing zombies made it difficult. It was hard to blend into the crowd when you grew up as the Lead Scientist's daughter.

"Hey, Edda!" said a lanky zombie munching on a bag of popbrain.

"So sorry about your mom," consoled an elderly zombie wearing a mildewy pink dress. She was gazing at me above her bifocals.

"Zombies sure seem to like you around here," said Bram teasingly.

I frowned. "Yeah, well, I used to be pretty easygoing, believe it or not."

"Brains! Brains for sale! You know you're craving braaains!" Brainmongers wearing rubber aprons, visors, and hairnets promoted their goods to the zombies lumbering by. They used large push brooms to sweep the piles of pollution ash away from their stalls.

The work wasn't easy. Brainmongers had to smear thick gobs of scented balm called brain block beneath their nostrils to reduce the urges brought on by the smell of their own product. And the brains sure did smell delicious. My nostrils swelled with the aroma of neatly organized brain balls, brain hash, brain kebabs, braincicles, and other zombie favorites.

It was very difficult to avoid cravings, so I picked up the pace.

The street turned to the east as it joined up with the Circle of Willis—a central zombie gathering point and the best place in Deadmark for zombie-watching. Named after the very first corpse to rise out of its Ignorwegian grave, the Circle of Willis was jam-packed with zombies moaning in groups, conducting science experiments, snacking on brains, and snapping tourist pics of Zømborg Castle.

But most of all, zombies used the Circle of Willis for speaking their minds around the circle's centerpiece: a towering marble statue in the shape of a giant zombie hand. It was known as the Ur-Hand statue, a grand representation of Willis's hand reaching up from Ignorwegian dirt and giving rise to zombiekind.

Protesters and activists swarmed around the Ur-Hand statue. Some were in groups, others alone. Some had pro-science signs with slogans like *"SCIENCE IS GOOD: IT'S EMPIRICAL,"* while anti-science signs responded with slogans like *"THE RESULTS ARE IN: SCIENCE FEELS IFFY."*

I noted a few signs expressing concern for my mom, and the worst signs of all declared loyalty to Agonista. With these combating viewpoints blasting into each other and across the circle, Deadmark seemed more confused than I was. If that was even possible.

Bram became distracted by an elaborate inflatable model of Zømborg Castle held in the air by a group of zombies from the historic preservation society. He half-jogged after me to catch up, and as soon as he did, we were both stopped abruptly by an angry zombie shoving a large, jagged sign into our faces.

The sign read, *"SAVE THE HUMANS,"* scrawled in dripping red paint.

"Eating brains is mindless!" screamed the zombie. Half-chewed cockroach guts sprayed out of his mouth. Startled, Bram and I took a step back.

The angry zombie staggered over to a group of protesters near the base of the Ur-Hand statue. Known as ZETH (Zombies for the Ethical Treatment of Humans), they were the circle's most frequent protesters.

The ZETHs yelled at every zombie passerby. They wore black hoodies with *ZETH* printed on the back, along with their

logo: a brain with a slash through it. They waved signs with slogans like *"BRAINS ARE MURDER," "NO BRAIN NO PAIN,"* and *"COCKROACHES DON'T SCREAM."*

While holding their signs and chanting, the ZETHs continually loaded their mouths with squirming, chittering cockroaches that they stored in sacks slung across their shoulders.

Long before Willis crawled out of his grave, Ignorwegian pollution had killed off all the animals in Ignorway and present-day Deadmark. All the animals, that is, except for the small creatures cultivated by my former lab partner in her filtered undersea garden, and the ever-resilient cockroach.

Most zombies only have a taste for human brains, but ZETHs have somehow trained themselves to tolerate cockroach brains. The problem for ZETHs was that cockroach brains were so tiny, they had to be eaten nonstop for the protesters to avoid starvation.

"This is so stupid," I muttered to Bram. He didn't respond. He was captivated with disgust at the sight of so many live cockroaches being devoured at once.

Even if I agreed with the protesters—which I don't, because, obviously, humans are NOT equal to zombies—eating cockroaches is completely impractical. It's unrealistic to force yourself to eat that many bugs constantly throughout the day. Unrealistic, not to mention revolting.

I stepped forward with a finger raised, ready to give them a few of my own thoughts. But before I had the chance to get a word in, a zombie brainmonger wheeled past with a brain-filled delivery cart.

The poor zombie had no idea what he was walking into.

Like a determined but slow-moving pack of wolves, the ZETHs lurched toward the cart of brains and began throwing and splattering them across nearby buildings and along the street.

A splash of brain juice whipped across my face and Bram's. Bram shrieked in disgust. I grunted with approval.

Most of the time, zombies are among the most sophisticated creatures in the world. We can be quite highbrow and intellectual. However, when it comes to brains, we get very single-minded.

When brains are arranged neatly on orderly shelves or in brainmonger stands, we can usually control ourselves. But it's another story entirely when they start getting tossed around and plopping on the ground.

For all the zombies in the area, the sound and the smell were too much to handle. All of them became instantly and completely possessed by the need to gobble them up.

All of them...including me.

My mouth watered and my eyes bulged at a particularly

bulbous knob of brain just laying there by my foot on the bone-paved road. The smell was overpowering.

"Brains?" I said to Bram, scooping a handful of squishy, tasty, slightly jiggly goo into my mouth.

"No, Edda," said Bram. "This isn't the time for a snack."

He put both hands on my shoulders and directed me away from the chaos. I wiped brain fluid from my chin and tried to stop the urge to go back for more.

"Brains are a terrible thing to waste..." I mumbled.

Turning a corner, the sight of the Glob Theater at the end of the road didn't help my state of mind. The theater was built to resemble a big, round, delicious glob of human brain.

When we reached the large double doors in front, Bram took his hands off my shoulders and cupped them around his mouth. "Yo, Rick!" he called out.

After a few seconds, the doors flung open and our faces lit up with the bluish glow emanating from an enchanted floating skull. Rick had a big grin framed by a pencil mustache above and a soul-patch beard below.

"Well, well, well," he said, noticing the brain juice splattered

on Bram's face and smeared on mine. "There has been much throwing about of brains, I see."

Rick looked us over with a mischievous glint in his eye socket.

I must have been panting with brain fever, because Rick chuckled and said, "It appears that Edda has brains on her mind."

Bram smiled nervously. "Ha, uh, yeah," he said. "She's a little distracted right now."

"Get in here, both of you," said Rick, floating behind us to corral us inside. "Before Edda forgets her manners."

After I had calmed down and Bram and I had cleaned up, the three of us made our way through the Glob's main entrance lobby and down the curved hallway to the wardrobe room behind the stage.

As Bram and I walked and Rick floated, I tried explaining my plan to Rick. He listened carefully, but he wasn't exactly convinced I knew what I was doing. It was hard to blame him.

"I'm not sure if your plan will work," he said. "But I love hijinks, and this sounds like excellent hijinks."

As I continued explaining, we passed offices and backstage

rooms filled with bustling Play Things—the troupe of child actors who performed at the Glob. They were building props, hemming costumes, and fine-tuning scripts.

Two of them ran toward us in the hallway. One wore the mask of an ogre, the other the mask of a hobgoblin. They both wore black shrouds beneath their masks, which was customary attire for Play Things who weren't in costume for a performance. I have always assumed the Play Things were zombie children, but the truth is, I've never seen one without a mask.

"Careful, kids!" Rick scolded good-naturedly as the Play Things giggled on past. "You're going to run over our guests!"

"Uh, did one of them just fart?" asked Bram, causing the Play Things to giggle all the more.

The Glob Theater's hallway walls displayed large photographs of past performances, most of them adaptations of Ignorwegian plays and films, tailored to the zombie audience.

Most of the plays were Ignorwegian in origin because, centuries ago, Rick had gotten his start in Ignorway as a full-bodied human playwright, actor, and comedian. At some point he told the wrong joke about the wrong Enchantress, and *POOF!* He was cursed to exist as a glowing, floating skull for the rest of eternity.

After his transformation, Rick worked as a silent prop in Ignorwegian theater whenever a play required a skull. Once

Deadmark was founded, he moved here to start the Theater Is Dead theater company and build the Glob Theater. A large, circular building with a stage at its center, the Glob Theater was a direct replica of the one Rick had led in Ignorway.

At last, we reached the Glob's wardrobe room and its overflowing racks, trunks, boxes, and drawers of clothing and costumes. In the far corner, I had arranged a woolly mammoth costume to form my grave. It wasn't the cold, mulchy dirt that I was used to sleeping in, but it did the trick.

After tossing my tool belt onto my makeshift grave, the three of us headed to the human clothing section.

Generally speaking, zombie clothes are basically the same as human clothes, just a lot more ragged and torn. But Rick didn't collect just any human clothes—he took great pleasure in collecting the silliest, wackiest specimens of human attire he could find. The ridiculous outfits were a hit in Rick's many comedies that made fun of human culture.

And he'd been doing it for so long, he had stockpiled a seemingly unlimited supply of human costume options. There were so many outfits and accessories to consider, we decided to each take a corner of the room to dive in and search for inspiration.

"Remember, guys, the zanier the better," I reminded them. From a trunk I pulled bedazzled boots, a police officer uniform, a sundress. I carefully considered them all, but they weren't quite right. "We need a human outfit that will really convince them that I'm nothing like the old Edda."

After a few minutes, Bram held up a pair of shiny purple platform shoes. They were intriguing, but not the winners. I shook my head.

Rick used his glowing blue head to illuminate a puffy green prom dress hanging on a rack. He gave me an inquiring look. I shook my head again.

"What in the world?" Bram asked. "Do humans actually wear these?" He was holding up a pair of rainbow socks with compartments for each toe, but my attention was elsewhere.

"Wait," I said. A wild smile ignited my face. I knew it immediately. I had found my human disguise.

Pulling it out from the trunk, I held it up for Bram and Rick to see. It was a coral-colored, body-length fleece blanket with sleeves and a hood. Nothing could possibly make me look less like myself.

"It's hideous," said Rick, awestruck. "I love it."

"I could never have imagined something so ridiculous," said Bram. "Not in my wildest dreams."

"Bram, my friend," I said with a smirk, "there are more things in this universe than you've ever even dreamed of."

CHAPTER FIVE

METHOD OR MADNESS?

I smell clouds of gas, it's CO_2,
it smells like doom, for me and you…
And I think to myself…what a blundering world.

So there I was three nights later, singing and twirling toward the entrance of Zømborg Castle's historic council room.

Squeak sat in his harness on Gibber's back as they both glared out from the doorway. With frowns on and machetes out, they looked scary and dangerous. But they didn't dare mess with me. Not in this outfit.

In a coral sleeved blanket and a blonde human wig with swoopy bangs, I must have resembled some kind of floppy beauty pageant starfish.

I winked up at Squeak, and then at Gibber. With a ballerina's leap, I bounded into the council room. Just as he had for the past three nights, Gibber stepped back to let me pass, as if whatever I had might be contagious.

As I frolicked away, I could hear Gibber mumbling incoherently, to which Squeak replied, "That's right, Gib. Not worth getting in the way of that one." Squeak was the only zombie who could understand Gibber's low-pitched, groaning mumbles.

While experimenting with various approaches to acting like an erratic human, I seemed to get the best reactions by singing zombie parodies of popular Ignorwegian music. I had picked up some choruses and verses from comedy performances by Rick and the Play Things.

Verses such as the one I sang now as I traipsed through the room:

I can't wish upon a star,
I have no idea where they are…
Everything in the sky is blocked from view…

Crooning and spinning past stately stone and bone columns, I made my way toward the seven members of the Elected Council sitting at a long banquet table at the front of the council room. As usual, they were gulping bubbly brain fluid and slurping down an extravagant assortment of brains.

Against the wall beside the banquet table, Agonista sat on a makeshift throne of human bones wearing her customary black turtleneck. She had a finger in her right ear as she spoke sternly into the earpiece in her left ear.

It was jarring to see her in this dignified room surrounded by banners depicting science symbols like microscopes, DNA strands, and bubbling beakers—things I knew Agonista didn't honor or believe in.

Beside her, on a much lower chair, a squat and bald zombie named Cabbagio calmly sipped on brain fluid in a plastic martini glass. He wore a threadbare monkish robe that was clearly meant to resemble the Elected Council robes—even though he was neither on the council nor elected. He wore multicolored gemstone rings on his fingers, and a large gemstone chunk dangled around his neck.

It wasn't surprising that Agonista had appointed Cabbagio to be her Chief of Staff even though he had no government experience. Not only was he the treasurer of Agonista's companies, he also held deeply superstitious and unscientific beliefs, which meant he fit right in with her anti-science ways.

For instance, for the past few days, I had heard Cabbagio

bragging about his gemstones. He called them Power Gems and he had picked them up from brain hunters returning from Ignorway. For whatever reason, he was convinced they possessed supernatural powers.

As part of my human act, I had pretended to be interested in the so-called Power Gems, but really I think "Sham Rocks" would be a much more accurate name. Cabbagio couldn't tell I was faking it, though—he actually tried to sell some to me and get me to sell them to my friends. I politely declined.

In addition to being Agonista's Chief of Staff, Cabbagio happened to be the dad of Nerida, my former lab partner. But they couldn't be more different. Nerida built her life around the rock-solid knowledge provided by the scientific method, while Cabbagio seemed to believe anything, regardless of its source.

As I belted out the second verse of "I Can't Wish Upon a Star," I heard a squeak of protest from within my hood. It was Bram, hiding in his bat form. "Edda, I think your performance is very believable," he said. "But how about we take a break from the singing for a bit?"

Bram only listened to death metal, so my choice of music—and my terrible singing—was very offensive to his sensitive bat ears.

I ignored Bram as I pranced with ridiculous flair to the corner of the council room. Like an attentive gargoyle, I perched on a stone bench and took in the scene.

The members of the Elected Council were solely focused on the bottles of high-end bubbly brain fluid and mountains of various types of gourmet cerebrum, cerebellum, lobe, and cortex that spilled over their table. It was an expensive and grandiose spread that only someone as rich as Agonista could afford.

The brains looked delicious, but, thankfully, I couldn't smell them. To avoid becoming distracted by serious cravings, I had applied brain-block balm under my nostrils before heading to the council room.

I clicked my tongue in disgust as I surveyed the specks and splashes of brain spattered across the Elected Council's traditional robes. "How far the Elected Council has fallen," I whispered to Bram.

While the Elected Council remained fully distracted by their food and drink, Squeak and Gibber loomed menacingly near the entrance to dissuade any journalist, scientist, or potentially unreceptive member of the public from entering.

When my mom was the Lead Scientist, Elected Council meetings were completely open to the public. She even opened the doors to visiting dignitaries from science-minded places like Franke and Morassia. And while Deadmark's citizens could still *technically* enter the council room under Agonista's rule, not many would dare confront Squeak and Gibber.

The rows of seats in front of the Elected Council were not nearly as full as they used to be, but scattered among the empty seats were a couple dozen zombies who bought into Agonista's worldview.

One of them had a sign reading "*SCIENCE IS BAD FOR BUSINESS.*" Another wore a tinfoil hat and seemed to be staring off into space. Tinfoil hats were customary Ignorwegian apparel. They believed the hats blocked out electromagnetic waves that zombies might use to control their minds. Of course, in reality, we didn't care about their minds. We just wanted their brains.

I had never seen a zombie wearing one before, and I couldn't possibly guess what his unscientific motivations might be.

Some of the zombies in the council room just sat and stared at Agonista with starstruck eyes, as if she were some kind of movie star.

Shaking my head, I hopped down from the bench to get closer to the Elected Council, hoping I could collect some information. Singing and humming to myself, I slowly skipped past them. For the most part, they remained fixated on their brainy bounty, but a few members turned their heads and gave me puzzled looks.

"Shame," said one, with bits of brain soufflé flying out of

her mouth. "The poor zombie is so beside herself, she thinks she's a human."

"Mmm, yes," said another, with brain fluid dripping down his chin. "Grief has eaten away her young, fragile mind."

After three nights of my performance, the Elected Council came to believe that I wasn't my old self. But it wasn't them I was really trying to trick. My aunt was the real target.

I turned my attention to Agonista as she took a sip of something from a single-use plastic cup. She looked inside, saw it was empty, and then casually tossed it over her shoulder.

"Where are we? *Rancidia*?" I asked Bram. "It's disgusting. And why is she on a throne? Deadmark is a democracy. She's not the queen. She might as well just shred the ReConstitution."

"Easy, Edda," Bram squeaked from my hood. "You're supposed to be odd and harmless, remember? Not angry and intimidating."

Agonista silenced the room with a sharp clap of her hands. "OK, Cabbagio," she said. "Let's take care of some official business." Her hefty wireless earpiece not only looked ridiculous, but also gave her voice a staticky, metallic quality. Surely she could afford a better model.

Cabbagio pulled out a laptop from behind his small chair and turned it on. "Yes, ma'am!" he declared enthusiastically as his ringed fingers danced over his keyboard.

"Are all members of the Elected Council present?" A sly smile crawled across Agonista's face as she peered over at the Elected Council's banquet table. Right on cue, Squeak and Gibber allowed a delivery zombie to enter the council room with a cart that, conveniently enough, was spilling over with more brains.

Council members responded to Agonista's question, but their greedy, bulging eyes remained glued to the brain cart.

"Right…"

"Sure, sure."

"Mmhmm."

One of them had already overindulged and lay with her head down on the table. Squeak climbed down from his harness and walked over to the non-responding zombie. With a mischievous grin, he prodded her with a baseball bat.

The zombie shot her hand into the air with a pathetic groan. "Present," she grumbled.

"Excellent," said Agonista. "Cabbagio, let the official record show that the entire Elected Council is present and attentive."

Cabbagio nodded as he clacked away on his keyboard. Agonista continued. "Deadmark was built on a rich tradition of science and the pursuit of knowledge." She gestured dismissively to the banners on either side of her. "But it's also built on rich deposits of oil…"

Agonista paused and glanced at the Elected Council to see if her words were getting a reaction. Sadly, the council members were too focused on gorging themselves to pay attention.

"As an amazingly successful business-zombie, I know a good opportunity when I see it," Agonista continued. "The ReConstitution was written over a century ago. Perhaps it could use some tweaks to make things a little more…*profitable*."

While like-minded zombies clapped and hooted from their seats, I struggled to hold back a yelp of horror.

"I can't believe she's so evil," I said to Bram. "If she's trying to hide what she's up to, she's not doing a very good job!"

Apparently, I was a little too loud. Agonista turned her cold, sunglasses-hidden gaze toward me.

"Edda, my darling niece," she said in the manner of a vampire speaking to a jugular vein. The metallic tinge to her voice made her sound all the more menacing.

I muttered to Bram: "I may be her niece, but this is less than nice."

Flashing a wide, delirious smile, I skipped closer to Agonista.

When I arrived before her false throne, I curtsied with my sleeved blanket and asked as innocently as I could muster: "Yes, Auntie?"

She took me in with one eyebrow crooked over her sunglasses. It was rare for me to be this close to her. Even for a zombie, her skin looked crumbling and unhealthy. Apparently unchecked greed wasn't great for the complexion.

"I only ask this because I love you," she lied. "Why are you dressed like this? Why are you singing and dancing and acting strangely? Are you still grumpy about your missing mommy?"

"If you think I look weird on the outside," I replied, "you wouldn't believe how messed up I feel on the inside."

"I can't possibly begin to know what that means," growled Agonista.

"Remember," Bram squeaked in my ear. "We need her to trust you."

"Yes!" I cried. "I meant to say: profits, profits, profits! Money is the best, right? You can buy so many things with it." And then under my breath, I added: "Entire countries, for instance."

"Quite right," said Agonista uncertainly. Then, turning to Cabbagio as if I wasn't there, she said, "This blanket situation is quite strange, but at least she's no longer moping around and mourning in those gloomy black clothes."

Agonista faced the council room seats and raised her voice

to make sure everyone could hear her. "Edda, my poor, grief-stricken niece! I miss my sister, too, I really do. We'll never know why she ran away, so let's just try to forget about it, OK?"

To avoid yelling in anger, I twirled and sang:

Ha-zy...it's hazy from all the pollution...
It's ha-zy...hazy wherever we go...
For so long, we've polluted as much as we wanted,
and now each day, we watch those smog layers grow.

"Ahem," said Cabbagio, trying to find his words. "Young Edda, it seems as though you're reeling due to recent events, but you really shouldn't be taking it so hard. I mean, zombies go missing all the time."

Without thinking, I skipped toward Cabbagio like a heat-seeking rocket. "Of course!" I yelled, clenching my fist in front of his sweaty face. "It happens *all* the time. Zombies go missing, morals go missing. We're always losing things around here..."

Cabbagio chortled nervously. "Haha! What a sharp sense of humor. You remind me of my daughter."

Agonista wasn't as good-natured about my comments. She slammed her fist onto the arm of her throne.

"That's enough, Edda!" she shrieked. She took a breath to

compose herself. "We all need to move on and do what's best for Deadmark. Acting out is not going to help anyone."

Bram whispered in my ear. "Easy, Edda. Don't lose your patience."

"The sooner you start to think of me as your Lead Scientist,"

Agonista continued, with an evil smile, "the better it will be for everyone."

I closed my eyes and took the deepest breath I could. Bram was right. I needed them to think of me as non-threatening.

"Yes, Aunt Agonista," I said, choking down all of my pride. "I will do my best to obey you."

With a half-hearted fist pump, I added, "Yay, money."

"That's a good niece," sneered Agonista.

I made a dramatic bow and slowly moonwalked away. I kept my eyes on Agonista and Cabbagio, waiting for the right moment. As soon as they were distracted, I darted behind a large stone-and-bone pillar and out of their vision.

"Gah!" I whispered to Bram, crouching low and peeking to the side of the pillar at Agonista. "I almost blew my cover. For now, I'll have to hold my tongue, and hope my heart doesn't break in the process."

Bram and I were close enough to hear Agonista address Cabbagio. "I do not trust my niece," she sneered. My moonwalking, pillar-ducking maneuver had worked—Agonista assumed I had left the council room. "One minute she seems to be on my side, and the next she's railing against me. Her unpredictable behavior makes me worry she'll do something drastic."

Just then, Argo, who was Cabbagio's son and Nerida's brother, walked past Squeak and Gibber. He gave them a friendly nod and entered the council room. Squeak and Gibber didn't seem to care.

Tall, athletic, and handsome, Argo fashioned his white zombie hair into small dreadlocks. He had always been a little hot-tempered, but as far as I knew, he was a pretty good guy.

He wore a scruffy blazer with a crest featuring a lightning bolt. This was the standard uniform at Sourbone University Prep, where Argo goes to school with the Frankenstein's Monsters in Franke.

Like Deadmark and Gormany, Franke is also a science-positive country, but the Franke scientific tradition is much more focused on electric necromancy. Go figure.

"Ah," said Cabbagio to Agonista. He rubbed his gemstone

necklace as he spoke. "Argo's arrival gives me a thought. I am certain my daughter, Nerida, can get to the bottom of Edda's behavior. They used to be very close."

Cabbagio turned his attention to his approaching son. "Argo!" he cried. "Do you, by chance, know where your sister is?"

"She's probably doing science experiments in her lab," he said. "Or tending to her undersea garden." He shrugged. "That's all she ever does."

"That brings up an interesting point," said Agonista with a hand on her chin. "Cabbagio, your daughter is awfully preoccupied with science. Are you certain we can trust her?"

"Oh, yes, we can trust her," he said. "She's skeptical now, but I'm sure she will eventually come around to your modern style of leadership."

Agonista nodded warily. Cabbagio smiled as he pulled out his smartphone. "I'll send her a text and request her presence."

After thumbing his phone, Cabbagio addressed his son. "Now, Argo," he said. "I assume you've come to say your goodbyes before you head back to Franke for summer school."

"Yep," said Argo. "I wanted to wish our new Lead Scientist the best of luck. It can't be easy taking over under such bizarre circumstances."

"Why, thank you, young Argo," said Agonista with a creepy smile. "If those Frankenstein's Monsters don't fill your mind with too much nonsense, you can come back to Deadmark to join my leadership team."

"Wow," said Argo. "It would be a privilege to serve the Lead Scientist of Deadmark." It was so sad to see Agonista's lies and deceit fully hoodwink a zombie I had known for years.

"Before you go, Son, I have some advice." Cabbagio cleared his throat and took a deep breath before continuing. "Sprinkle salt across the threshold before you enter any new building. Avoid mirrors and ladders, and—oh yeah!—cats aren't extinct in Franke, so avoid black cats, too. In fact, don't even think about black cats."

"I don't think I can stomach much more of this," I whispered to Bram.

"Above all else, my son, to thine own self, voodoo," said Cabbagio. He reached behind his chair and pulled out a clumsily made doll that vaguely resembled Argo. It had little dreadlocks and everything. "Whenever you get stressed, give this doll a shoulder massage. It will help you relax. I'm telling you, it works wonders."

Argo politely accepted the doll, but his mouth was pinched with skepticism.

Cabbagio looked past Argo. "Nerida!" he yelled. Everyone turned toward the entrance, including me. I felt Bram climb on top of my head to get a look.

My heart sank at the sight of my one-time lab partner. As always, Nerida's large, confident eyes were covered by laboratory goggles. Her lush and curly pink hair was threaded with seaweed and coral and adorned with the occasional seashell.

Nerida stood outside the council room's entrance dripping wet, as if she had just emerged from underwater. With a signal from Agonista, Gibber stepped aside to allow her to pass, along with the trail of water that followed her in.

I ducked low behind the pillar so Nerida wouldn't see me. After hearing her pass by, I peeked back out to see her wave hello to her brother and then stop in front of Cabbagio and Agonista. She adjusted the sack on her shoulder, which was overflowing with bushels of colorful aquatic plants and organisms.

If she was intimidated by Agonista, she didn't show it.

"What's up, Dad?" she asked. "You texted? I was about to run some errands."

Agonista spoke before Cabbagio could. "Yes, Nerida," she said, with false kindness. "Your friend Edda is acting very strangely. And there may be a method to her madness, if you know what I mean. Since you know her so well, perhaps you can find out what's troubling her."

Nerida blinked at Agonista in silence.

"We can't possibly help 'fix' Edda's problem if we don't know what it is," said Agonista. She framed menacing air quotes around the word "fix" with her long, bony fingers. "Do you understand?"

"Edda and I are not as close as we once were," said Nerida, her voice steady. "But I would never spy on her. Her mom is missing and I'm sure she's hurting very badly. I'll talk to her and ask her if there's anything I can do to help, if that's what you're asking."

Cabbagio chuckled nervously. "Ah, yes, that's what she meant, of course. Please, just tell us what she says, OK?"

Argo butted in. "Just don't let her trick you, sister," he said. "The vampires down in Gormany may have taught her how to hypnotize."

Nerida rolled her eyes. "I can take care of myself, thanks. And besides—everyone knows zombies can't be hypnotized."

She turned to walk back to the council room's entrance. I crouched down even lower so she wouldn't see me as she passed my pillar.

"Nerida!" Agonista called after her. "Your loyalty is of the utmost importance. Deadmark relies on it."

"Uh, sure," said Nerida. When she reached my pillar, she bent down and whispered, "Meet me in my lab in an hour, princess. I have something to give you. Nice hair, by the way."

My face burned with anger. I couldn't help it. "Do not call me 'princess'!" I hissed.

Ever since my mom was elected Lead Scientist, Nerida had teased me for being "royalty" and a "princess." It got under my skin then, and it still does now.

Nerida smiled victoriously. She loved getting a reaction out of me. She stood up to walk away, but then popped her head back down.

"Oh, one more thing," she said with a smile. "When you come over, please ask Bat Boy to hang somewhere else."

CHAPTER SIX
ZOMBIE, OR NOT TO BE

G reen rain stung my cheeks as I climbed up the stone steps that led to Nerida's lab. The wind and rain were particularly harsh here, as the tower hovered directly over the Undead Sea.

However, right now, it wasn't exactly rain. It was more like pure acid. This happened from time to time when poisoned pollution clouds crept over from Ignorway. When it splashes down, it dissolves clothes, erodes buildings, and burns faces.

But I kept my hood down despite the stinging. I welcomed anything to distract me from my crumbling world, no matter how painful.

I approached the door to Nerida's lab and glanced to my

right. I felt a buzz of surprise when I squinted through the rain to the Lead Scientist's quarters on the opposite end of the castle. A shadow had shifted across the lit window of my old graveroom.

If Agonista was with the Elected Council in the council room, who could be in the Lead Scientist's quarters? And why were they in my room?

Goosebumps swept across the back of my neck. It felt creepy and violating to have my childhood graveroom overtaken by Agonista and her secret guest. I wished Bram were here to help me speculate about this, but he had reluctantly fluttered back to the Glob Theater to honor Nerida's wishes.

The gloomy notes of Zømborg Castle's clock snapped me out of my thoughts. With a twitchy feeling in my stomach, I tore my eyes from my graveroom window and pulled open the heavy stone door to Nerida's lab.

I walked inside, wiped the green rain off of my face, and wrung out my sopping sleeved blanket as best I could. I took my blonde wig off and laughed at its new green highlights, courtesy of the acid rain. *Better that wig than my hair*, I thought to myself, tossing it with a wet *SLAP!* onto a counter.

After composing myself, I looked around. The first thing I noticed was the lab's emptiness. Nerida was nowhere in sight.

The circular lab walls were lined with shelves of beakers

and glass jars filled with sea herbs, a variety of shells, and the skeletons of extinct sea creatures, including crabs, small sharks, otters, and sea turtles.

Garlands of seaweed were hung about the ceiling and threaded through the shelving. The lab had a pleasant underwater feel, like a cozy room in a sunken ship.

This is Nerida's happy place, and at one point, it was mine, too. Many of the jars and specimens lining the shelves triggered happy memories, mementos from our days together cheerfully documenting, analyzing, and discussing our scientific findings.

My eyes stopped on a dusty gold trophy, high up on one of the shelves. I felt a pang of sadness. It was the award for first place that Nerida and I had won in the national youth science fair two years ago. We had won the top prize for our creation of a brain-eating aquatic plant that we named Hebenon.

Winning that trophy was the height of our friendship and scientific collaboration. Then, as seems inevitable in this world, it all came crashing down.

With the enormous dangers facing our generation, I had begun to feel that studying plants was not the best use of my time. I drifted away from marine botany and accepted a scholarship to study at Bittenberg University Prep.

At Bittenberg, I could learn a completely new Gorman science tradition. I could learn about lots of shiny, fancy topics like the hypnotic arts (mind control), hematology (the study of blood), and chiropterological transmogrify (bat transformation). The list goes on and on.

Of course, I didn't know if Gorman science was better or more helpful than marine botany. But at least it was different.

So, I moved to Gormany and left it all behind—Nerida, our experiments, and, apparently, our friendship. I don't think she's ever forgiven me.

With a sigh, I grabbed a step stool and climbed up to peer at the highest shelf. I took down a mermaid skull, stepped down, and placed it on the table. I went back to the empty spot on the shelf and opened a hidden hatch. The opening revealed a hollowed-out portion of the stone castle wall.

Inside were two corked glass bottles filled with a glittery pink goo. The word *HUMANIZER* was scrawled on each bottle in black marker. So she *hadn't* gotten rid of it.

Staring at the bottles, I tried to remember if our batch had yielded two or three bottles. Was one missing? If so, could it have been the dose that allegedly humanized my mom?

After pulling one of the bottles from the secret hiding spot, I closed the hatch and placed the mermaid skull back on the shelf.

Holding the bottle up to my face, I examined the shimmering, bright-pink substance inside. Tiny specks sparkled within.

It looked harmless enough, but with one swig of this goop, I could turn into a human. Just like that.

At this point, being a zombie wasn't that great…could being a human really be that much worse? With Agonista running Deadmark, were zombies any better than humans anymore?

"Zombie, or not to be?" I said out loud, twirling the mutagen in my fingers. "It's quite the question. Would becoming a human end the stresses of zombiehood and my outrageous bad luck? Could life as a human be better than my death as a zombie?"

"Who are you talking to?" came Nerida's voice from the doorway behind me. Quickly, I slipped the mutagen bottle into a fleece pocket. I whipped around and began dancing and belting out the first human song that popped into my head.

I'm stingin' in the rain, just stingin' in the rain!
What a torturous feeling, I'm hurting again!

Nerida's annoyed expression delivered a ripple of humiliation. "Are you done?" she asked, one hand propped impatiently on her hip. "You can knock it off now, I know you're faking it."

I trailed off the song lyrics, slowed my dancing to a halt, and cleared my throat. "Yes," I said. "I'm faking it. But so is everyone else. Deadmark has become a prison filled with zombies I can't trust."

"If Deadmark is a prison," said Nerida, unloading her canvas bag, "then the whole world is." She carefully arranged various bottles of chemicals and elixirs on her lab table.

"That may be true," I said pulling up a stool. "But with Agonista in charge, Deadmark feels like one of the worst."

Nerida was making direct eye contact with me, like she was my mom or something. "Look—I don't know what all this is," she said, gesturing snidely to my outfit. "And I don't know what the weird human act is all about, but it all seems like a very unscientific approach to solving your problems."

"The way things are going, I'm not sure if I believe in anything anymore...not even science," I said. Then, almost under my breath, I added: "Maybe I never believed in science."

Had I slapped her in the face, Nerida would not have looked more offended. "Well I guess you lied, then! I mean, you took an oath!" she snapped. "An oath that we wrote together!"

It was true. When we were lab partners, Nerida and I co-wrote a scientific oath that we promised to stand by, no matter what:

Doubt that the stars are fairy dust.
Doubt that the sun won't cease.
But don't doubt science is the key
to future zombie peace.

I really did believe the oath when we wrote it, but now it felt silly.

"That was forever ago, Nerida," I said. "We had no idea what the future had in store. We didn't know what we were talking about."

Nerida slammed her fist down on the table. "Who are you?" she demanded. "This isn't the Edda I used to know. Next you're going to tell me that there's no such thing as good and bad—that it's all in our heads."

She crouched down on the ground and began angrily rifling through one of the bottom cupboards.

"We used to be science partners," she said. "Our values were completely in sync, and then, out of nowhere, you just left."

"Listen," I said with a sigh. "I know you're mad at me for leaving—"

Nerida rocketed up from her crouched position and cut me off. "You don't get it, do you!?" she yelled, eyes bulging behind her goggles. "I'm not mad that you left. And I'm not mad that you wanted to expand your horizons."

She placed her hand on her forehead, sadness replacing her anger. "I'm mad that you didn't say goodbye. You didn't say anything. One day I woke up and you had just...vanished."

She was right. I didn't say goodbye. I couldn't. My fear was too much. I was worried what Nerida would think, how my decision would make her feel. I was convinced she would hate me, so I didn't even try.

Nerida bent down and came up holding a bag of what looked like dehydrated brain pellets. "What is going on with you, Edda? Your mom is missing and you haven't even talked to me about it. You haven't talked to me at all. We used to be best friends, remember?"

I wanted to tell Nerida everything. I wanted us to be best friends again and to ask her to help me fix it all. But I just stared at her blankly, thoughts of fear and embarrassment pulsing behind my eyes.

"Fine," she said. "Keep it all inside. I have to feed Hebenon. I was going to give you something, but forget it. You're free to do whatever you want. That's what you always do anyway."

Her pink hair whipped to the side as she turned briskly away and walked to the back of her lab. "Inviting you here was a mistake," she said. "Just keep singing and prancing around like an undomesticated human. I'm sure that will solve all your problems."

As she reached the back entrance, she grabbed her metal diving helmet off a hook and rushed outside and down the stone steps toward her undersea garden.

Seeing myself through Nerida's eyes made my face burn with shame. I looked down at my sleeved blanket and then at the green-tinged wig on the counter. Nerida would never have done this. She was always so smart and composed. Compared to her, I really was undomesticated.

Intense emotions bubbled inside my skull. As I paced back and forth, the feelings gained steam and began to change shape. Soon enough, my humiliation transformed into anger, and embarrassment became bitterness.

I picked up the sopping wig and slapped it back onto the counter. *How dare she judge me like that? How dare she make me feel like this on top of everything I'm going through?*

Darting to the back entrance, I grabbed my old diving helmet off its hook and bounded outside after her. The wind wailed as the waves slammed up against the castle. Two steps at a time, I hurtled downward to the violent sea.

It wasn't until I was halfway down that it hit me: All this time, Nerida had kept my diving helmet on its hook beside hers. It was as if she held it there awaiting my return.

At the bottom of the steps, Nerida's light blue aluminum motorboat rose and dipped in the raging black water. It was tied to a brass ring jutting out from the side of the castle.

Near the boat, thin but durable plexiglass formed a semi-circle barrier around the fresh, unpolluted water of Nerida's garden. The barrier stretched from the water's surface all the way to the seafloor, creating a cylinder of clean water protected from the black, churning poison of the Undead Sea.

We had designed this high-tech garden together, including the bubbling filters at the surface and the little floating LED balls of light that move throughout to provide artificial sunlight.

After fastening on my helmet and switching on its communication receiver, I splashed into the pure waters of the undersea garden. As my sleeved blanket swelled with water, it occurred to me that my choice in diving attire was less than ideal.

It was too late to reconsider, so I did my best to kick and thrash downward. I used my hands to pull myself down along immense strands of kelp that reached from the seafloor to the surface.

As I fought to gain momentum, little schools of minnows and squid flitted around my head to get a good look at their new visitor. Nerida's undersea garden had come a long way since I left for Gormany.

Below me, I could see Nerida feeding Hebenon. Along with the floating LED balls drifting around like ocean fairies, little blue and purple jellyfish billowed around Nerida's head. She was petting Hebenon with one hand and offering him a brain pellet with the other.

Hebenon peacefully munched away. His thick stalk grew out of the seafloor, connecting to a spherical head collared by feathery frills that bobbed and swayed in the current. He had no facial features save for a large, razor-tooth-filled mouth that smiled widely in between bites of brain.

The two of them were surrounded by Nerida's thriving, organized rows of multicolored aquatic plants and organisms— seaweed, fungi, sponges, coral, and more.

Hebenon caught my scent and chirped with delight. I was very upset, but I couldn't resist patting his head and greeting my co-creation. Hebenon nuzzled into my side. Nerida pretended to ignore me.

"Sure, OK," I said to Nerida through my helmet's receiver. "I've been acting strange, but you know what's even stranger? The world around us! At this point, zombies are no better than humans, and who cares, anyway? Soon enough, climate change will just turn us all to dust."

Nerida finally looked up at me. Even through her goggles and diving helmet, her sadness was obvious. "Look, I know things seem really bad right now." She was speaking slowly and calmly, as if restraining her emotion. "And I feel so sorry for what happened to your mom, but…"

"Sorry?!" I snapped. "It sounds to me like you'd rather judge me and my outfit than face the truth. The humans are destroying our world, and we're going down with them. We might as well go to a cemetery and crawl back into our graves for good!"

"To a cemetery?" Nerida asked in disbelief.

"Yes!" I cried. "To a cemetery!" Hebenon whimpered at my side. He clearly did not like that we were fighting.

"I really wish you were your old self again," said Nerida, her voice trembling slightly. "I'm sorry, Edda, you can spend your time roleplaying as a human, but I will not give up."

Nerida petted Hebenon's head to soothe him. "There is a way forward. I know there is. We have to trust in science. We can't lose hope."

I looked at Nerida's distraught face and felt terrible for all that I had said. Did I mean it? Was I still acting? I was mad at the world, lashing out, and I didn't feel in control of my words. I started off by acting like I had completely changed…was it possible it was no longer just an act?

"Nerida," I started. "I—"

"No," she said. "Stop right there. You've said enough." She

reached into her pocket and pulled out folded sheets of water-proof paper. Neatly written notes covered every inch.

"We wrote these lab notes together," she said. "They led to our creation of Hebenon and this entire undersea garden. I held on to them for sentimental reasons, to remember a time when we really got along, when we accomplished great things together."

Nerida handed me the notes. With a blank face and shaky hand, I took them from her.

"When you left for Gormany without saying goodbye, I was afraid that you didn't care at all. Now, after all you've said, it's clear that my fears were justified. You took off without saying a word, but I still held hope you'd come back and apologize, and maybe, someday, we'd resume our studies together. I guess I was wrong. Keep the notes if you want—I no longer want them."

In a flash, my old lab partner swam up to the surface with little jellyfish and minnows trailing behind. She left me and Hebenon alone at the bottom of the sea, surrounded by her well-loved, carefully cultivated garden.

Being underwater made it difficult to tell for certain, but before Nerida swam away, I could have sworn I saw tears in her eyes.

CHAPTER SEVEN

THE AUNT TRAP

I stormed down Cerebrum Street toward the Glob Theater, sheets of late-night acid rain cascading down. The stinging rain made very little difference to me. I had already maxed out on pain, and after being underwater, I was as wet as anyone could be.

In my rush to leave Nerida's lab, I had forgotten my blonde wig. Although I had the hood up on my sleeved blanket, some of my hair stuck out, and I knew it would be tinged with green for days.

After saying goodbye to Hebenon, I had swum up to the surface and walked up the steps to Nerida's lab. She was there pretending to organize a drawer of seashells, but I knew she was watching me from the corner of her eye.

She must have seen that I was still holding the lab notes, because she smirked a little as I passed. That's when I bolted out of there as fast as I could.

A blast of wind screamed in from the north-northwest. Lightning struck behind me, bleaching the sky with eye-splitting white light. A half second later, thunder roared. The sound and vibrations rolled through the streets and up my body.

But the storm didn't slow me down. The way I felt, it might as well have been coming from inside my brain.

It was the middle of the night, but the streets were deserted. The wind and rain were too much, forcing zombies to hide indoors and take cover from the harsh weather.

As I marched past the Ur-Hand statue, there were no tourists, no zombies doing science experiments, no protesters, no one yelling at each other. There was no one but me there to witness the marble hand reaching up from the ground and into the violent skies.

I noted that even the ZETHs, the most committed protesters, were taking a break. Absentmindedly, I wondered where they went when they weren't shoving signs in zombies' faces.

My sleeved blanket felt heavier than a suit of armor as I slopped onward through the rain. I leaped over a gushing stream of green water and stomped back down on the other side.

Without thinking, I reached into my pocket and pulled out the laminated lab notes. Staring at the tiny, handwritten words, I felt a wave of sadness.

I should have told Nerida what was happening with my mom. I should have given her the opportunity to help, instead of just shutting her out. And, before I left for Gormany, I should have said goodbye and explained myself. Or at least tried.

If anyone knew how brutal it felt to have a loved one vanish out of thin air, it was me.

Shoving the lab notes back into my pocket, I picked up the pace.

Another lightning bolt struck a turbine on the north side of the castle. Thunder rumbled overhead. The turbine wasn't spinning. Glancing around, I counted more motionless turbines in view than working ones. With a sigh, I leaned into the wind and rain.

Arriving at the large double doors of the Glob Theater, I flung them open without knocking. Rain gushed around me and across the stone lobby floor. I fought the wind to close the doors behind me, and after a moment's breath of rest, I turned around.

The lobby was empty, but I could hear voices coming from the theater on the other side of the lobby wall. Well, I could hear one voice in particular: Rick's.

I walked through the lobby doors and into the theater space.

Originally built to be an open-air theater, the audience area and stage have since been covered by large tarps to protect zombies from pollution flakes and acid rain. The flakes and rain have never really stopped, so the tarps have never come down.

Bram was leaning against the wall near the stage, browsing his smartphone. Large, round headphones covered his ears as he nodded his head in quick-paced rhythm to what was surely some sort of vampiric death metal beat. He was the only one in the otherwise empty audience.

Just like Rick's former theater in Ignorway, the Glob's main audience area had no seats. It was known as the pit, a place where zombies of all stripes watched plays together. Brainmongers, scientists, schoolteachers, brain hunters, you name it—everyone was welcome in the Glob's pit.

Lining the pit were balconies where fancy zombies like Agonista, Cabbagio, and the Elected Council would watch plays and sip their bubbly brain fluid. But my mom and I always preferred the pit—it's where we watched plays, even when she was Lead Scientist.

Rain pounded down on the tarps above as I made my way to Bram. The tarps billowed and shook in the wind, but they did their job of keeping the pit mostly dry.

On stage, Rick rushed into the faces of rehearsing Play

Things as he blared out acting critiques and instructions.

The Play Things were dressed in ragtag zombie versions of tropical outfits: frayed and shabby flower-print shirts, sarongs, cargo shorts, straw hats, and the like. On their faces, they wore cartoonish zombie masks bearing a variety of pained and terrified expressions.

Behind the actors rehearsing their scene, a group of Play Thing stagehands were constructing some kind of bizarre dog puppet with slimy tentacles coming out of it. The puppet sat in a puddle of oozing black goo.

"You're forgetting the golden rules of acting!" Rick yelled at the actors. Streaks of blue light trailed behind him as he whizzed around the stage. "Don't be too emotional, but don't be too tame. Just be natural. If I had arms and legs and a body, I'd do it myself!"

Bram was humming along to his music when I slumped

against the wall next to him. My sleeved blanket made a squelching sound against the plaster.

"Edda!" he said, startled. He removed his headphones from his ears. "You're soaked!"

"Yeah," I said, watching green liquid drip off of me and trickle down toward the stage. "I went underwater and tried to dry off in a hurricane. It didn't work out very well."

Bram reached into his backpack and pulled out a coffin-patterned hoodie. "Here, dry off with this."

"Thanks," I said. I wrung out the sleeved blanket as best as I could and dabbed Bram's hoodie against my face.

"How did it go with Nerida?" he asked. "What did she want to give you?"

"Oh, it went great!" I yelled with fake enthusiasm. Everyone on stage turned in my direction. "Everything is great! I said all the right things. We had a great conversation."

I pulled out the bottle of humanizer mutagen and clutched it in Bram's face. "And look what I found! The whole experience really got me thinking about death and life, zombies and humans, and this wacky world we all share."

Bram took a step back and then reached toward the bottle to lower my hand. "Whoa, um, are you OK, Edda?" he asked with a forced chuckle. "First of all, you're gnashing your teeth again. Secondly…does that bottle say 'humanizer'?"

I cleared my throat and forced my own chuckle. I placed the bottle back in my pocket. "Sure does," I said, as casually as I could.

Bram took a deep breath. "So, did Nerida notice if any of it was missing from her lab? I mean, besides the bottle in your pocket."

I didn't answer immediately. I could see Bram's mind whirring as he puzzled through my silence.

"Wait..." he said. "You didn't even ask her?"

"No, I didn't," I admitted. "I'm not sure if you've noticed, but I haven't exactly been thinking straight lately. But don't worry, Bram. I may be a little on edge, but I know a hawk from a handsaw, I can tell you that much."

Bram looked more concerned than ever. "Edda, that's the weirdest thing I've ever heard." He nervously rubbed the back of his head.

"It's an expression," I said with a false confidence that I couldn't commit to. "I think. Never mind. The point is, I'm only acting like I've lost my grip. I haven't jumped off the deep end quite yet." I couldn't commit to that statement either, so I added, "At least, I'm pretty sure."

"Edda, do you remember the oath I took on the castle wall... with the magnifying glass?" Bram asked cautiously. Before I could respond, Rick floated down from the stage.

"Everything good here, zombies and vampires?" he asked with theatrical flourish. Up on stage, the Play Things continued rehearsing without him. "Sorry about the commotion. I swear, those kids get on stage and forget the very basics of drama."

"We're OK," said Bram. And then, with a sideways glance, "I hope."

Rick whipped his skull around and yelled at the stage: "Romero! No improvising! Stick to the script, please."

Rick turned back to me and Bram. The Play Things giggled as the scolded actor performed a little jig of contempt aimed at Rick. But Rick didn't notice.

"Sorry," he whispered. "That kid seems to forget he's an actor and not a director." Rick shook his skull. "Anyway, do you have any updates, Edda?"

"Not really..." I said, dropping my head.

"Well, kind of really," said Bram. "Edda found so-called humanizer mutagen in Nerida's lab—possibly the same stuff that humanized her mom." And then after a pause: "And she brought some with her. Right now. In her pocket." He tried to give Rick a concerned look without me noticing, but I would have seen it from a mile away.

Rick's eye sockets expanded with alarm. "And why in the name of Deadmark did you bring such a thing to the Glob Theater? You're not planning to humanize Agonista, are you?"

"No, don't worry," I said, reasonably confident I was telling the truth. "I don't think that would solve anything. I mean, it wouldn't, right?"

"No, it wouldn't," said Bram. "Not even a little bit."

Bram put his hand on my shoulder. "Listen, Edda," he said calmly. "Maybe it's time we tried a different approach. Acting like a human doesn't seem to be working, and besides—it doesn't seem all that good for your mental health."

"You mean to tell me that dancing and singing like a human didn't solve all of your problems?" Rick asked sarcastically. "Now imagine that."

I laughed a little at Rick's joke, and my friends responded with their own nervous laughter. We were like a group of actors ourselves, doing a bad job of portraying a fun time.

"No, you're right," I said. "I'm sorry, guys. I've publicly humiliated myself for three nights now, and the only thing I've accomplished is making you two uncomfortable and somehow making Nerida even angrier with me."

"Don't mention it, Edda," said Bram. "You've had a rough few weeks, to put it mildly."

"You've been given a very raw deal," said Rick. "And coming from a floating skull, that should mean a lot."

"I know, but I have to stop dwelling on how bad things are. I need to find a way forward," I said, my eyes clamped tight

in concentration. "There has to be a way to know for sure if the thing in the coal mine is telling the truth…but what is it?"

I took several paces in a circle and put my hands in my hair as if I could physically pull out an idea. "I just wish we could hold a mirror up and reveal Agonista's evil deeds."

"That reminds me of what I tell my actors all the time," said Rick. "Theater is meant to hold a mirror up to reality. To show the audience the world as it really is."

Bram and I responded with blank expressions. "Sorry," said Rick. "That was off topic."

But then it hit me like a falling sandbag. "Apology not accepted!" I yelled, jumping into the air and again interrupting the rehearsal. "Because that's *exactly* what we'll do!"

Perplexed, Bram and Rick just stared back. "We'll use the play to show Agonista a mirror reflection of herself and the terrible things she has done. If she squirms in her seat, we'll know for sure that it's all true! And a whole theater of zombies will be there to see it—including the Elected Council."

"I love it!" cried Rick, bouncing up and down in the air.

"That's the kind of impactful theater we strive for here at the Glob. When the audience sees things for what they are, they will be changed forever. Some will feel fear, some will feel sorrow."

"Yes," I exclaimed. "And, if we do it right, at least one zombie will feel terrible guilt!"

"But the Play Things are already rehearsing a play," said Bram. "They'd only have a couple nights to memorize a completely new one."

"Maybe we don't need an entirely new play," I said, turning to Rick. "Could the Play Things handle a reworked scene or two?"

"Oh, yes," said Rick, twirling around with glee. "The Play Things are quite versatile. They can do horror, romance, comedy, horror-comedy, comedy-romance, or even romance-horror. We've grown tired of performing our musical rendition of *Day of the Dead Living* (even though it's a big hit), so tonight we are mixing it up and performing an adaptation of an Ignorwegian sci-fi story. I'm sure they'd be happy to work in some new material."

"Great," I exclaimed. "And what's the name of the play they're rehearsing?"

"The Play Things' play is *The Thing*," said Rick.

"The Play Things' play is the thing?" I asked, confused. "What 'thing'?"

"The play is called *The Thing*," explained Rick. "It's the story of a tropical research outpost that is terrorized by a virus from outer space that infects zombies. Nobody can tell who's a zombie and who's an alien imposter *pretending* to be a zombie. It's terrifying."

Rick turned around and nodded toward the tentacled dog puppet on stage. "It even mimics other creatures. The special effects team created this gooey puppet showing the alien in the middle of transforming into a dog," he said with a grimace. Right on cue, a Play Thing wearing a pumpkin mask pulled down on a rope, causing black goo to ooze beneath the dog-alien puppet and across the stage floor.

The black goo gave me an idea.

"That sounds perfect. The play *is* the thing!" I cried.

"Yes, Edda," said Bram. "We have established that this is a play version of *The Thing*."

"No, no, no," I laughed. "I mean, the play is just the thing to expose my aunt as a villain."

CHAPTER EIGHT

THE PLAY THINGS' PLAY IS *THE THING*

Two nights later, Bram and I watched from the pit as zombie after zombie shuffled into the Glob Theater. We found a place to stand that was close, but not too close, to Agonista's balcony seats on the right side of the stage.

Throughout the quickly filling playhouse, there was a buzz of anticipation for the new show from Rick and the Play Things. But no zombie anticipated this performance more than I did.

For the last couple nights, we had worked late into the day updating and rehearsing the new scene. Despite the long hours, I was able to get my first decent days of sleep in a while. It felt good to have a new plan to focus on, if only to distract my mind from dark, brooding thoughts.

I had changed out of my wet sleeved blanket and into my usual tattered jeans and a raggedy red flannel shirt. I wanted to shift the focus away from my odd behavior and wardrobe and direct all eyes toward the play.

Before my brain could register it, spiky twinges in my stomach let me know that I was watching Agonista take her balcony seat. She was followed by Cabbagio, and then Squeak and Gibber.

My hand instinctively wandered down to touch the bottle of humanizer mutagen in my pocket, and I quickly pulled it away.

Since taking mutagen from Nerida's lab, I had been conflicted about what to do with it. It's not like I could just throw it away. So, instead of risking it falling into someone else's ill-intentioned hands, I held on to it. I figured this was the best way to avoid a tragedy.

"I can't wait to see her reaction," whispered Bram as we both sneakily observed Agonista and her cronies. Agonista was scolding an usher as Gibber lowered Squeak into a balcony seat beside him. "I'm going to watch her as closely as I'd watch a thief."

"That's very appropriate," I said, "considering she's trying to steal my country."

I gasped when, out of nowhere, a pink-haired form swooped

in beside me. I gasped again when I found myself staring into Nerida's goggled eyes.

"I know you probably expected me to ignore you," she said. "But I don't like doing what's expected of me."

Nerida smiled at my shocked expression. "You took the lab notes. That's all I needed to confirm that somewhere, deep down, you still care about me…and you still believe in science."

She responded to my stunned silence with a grin. "Much better outfit, by the way," she said. "Far more practical."

With a deep breath, I tried to compose myself. I was very happy that Nerida was here, but I wasn't quite ready to admit it. "Welcome to the Glob Theater," I said, performing a grand, formal bow. "We've made some changes to the play…I'm excited to see your reaction."

Nerida squinted her eyes with suspicion. "What kind of changes?" she asked.

"Oh, we just punched it up a little," I said, pleased to have Nerida back on her heels. "But the real entertainment will come from my aunt's response. You should watch her as closely as you watch the play. The way she acts will be the most revealing performance of all."

Nerida glanced from me to my aunt and back again. "Your clothes might be better, but you're definitely still being weird."

Agonista cackled wildly from her balcony seat. She was

apparently getting a thrill out of whatever mindless story Cabbagio was whispering in her ear.

I looked around the nearly full theater. Zombies were laughing and chit-chatting as if everything were normal and fine. Many of them munched noisily on drippy handfuls of popbrain.

"Look how cheerful everyone is!" I said, tugging on my hair. "It's like they have completely forgotten about my mom."

"Well, just wait until the play gets going," whispered Bram. "They're in for a shock."

"You're right," I said. "Agonista, at least, won't be so happy then."

The house lights dimmed. I turned to the balcony where the Elected Council usually sits, but their seven seats were empty. This was extremely disappointing, and also very odd: The Elected Council hadn't missed a performance at the Glob for as long as I could remember.

Gesturing to the seven vacant balcony seats, I gave Bram a look of puzzled frustration. He shrugged and whispered, "They're probably too stuffed to walk away from the council room."

Suddenly, the curtains parted, and Rick floated to the front of the stage. With his natural bright blue illumination, he didn't require a spotlight. He gazed solemnly at the audience as the laughter and chatter quieted down.

"Who goes there!?" Rick's commanding voice boomed across the theater. "We ask this fundamental question of strangers, of our best friends, of even ourselves."

The crowd was utterly still. There wasn't so much as a groan.

"For how can we tell what lurks within the darkest corners of our skulls? How can we tell who we really are? How can we trust each other when it's so easy to deceive one another...to deceive ourselves?"

Rick basked in the theater's pin-drop silence. After a long pause, he continued. "We begin our story at a zombie research post in Fallapartica. Human-caused climate change has melted all the ice caps and transformed this once-frozen continent into a humid, scorching landscape."

A scattering of boos rose up from the crowd at the mention of humans and climate change. Not as many as I would have liked, but it was good to know that at least a few zombies still had their heads on straight.

Rick floated to the right side of the stage to lock eyes with Agonista. "But one of the scientists at the research post is not who they seem. Someone among them was not there for science," he said, with devilish flair. "No! Someone among them was only there for personal gain."

Rick maintained eye contact with Agonista, but she didn't move a muscle. Could she tell? Did she have a clue this performance was for her, a guilty audience of one?

"And it's worse!" cried Rick. "Someone among them may have been something utterly destructive and dreadful. Someone among them may have been…" Rick held the pause for full dramatic effect. He had them in the palm of his nonexistent hand. "…*a science-hating monster!*"

Rick hooted with glee as Agonista scratched her scalp, adjusted her earpiece, and slunk down in her seat. While some zombies booed, and a few cheered, all of them seemed eager to find out what Rick had in store.

"I present to you our adaptation of a play called *The Thing!*" Rick declared. "Just wait there and see what happens."

"I prefer to call it *The Aunt Trap*," I whispered to Bram, but loud enough so Nerida would hear.

Rick disappeared backstage and the curtains closed behind him. Zombies clapped politely, but the overall mood in the theater was distinctly tense.

As soon as the applause faded, the curtains opened and the stage lights turned on to reveal a set depicting the interior of a tropical research facility.

It was quite the scene: Several Play Things were sitting on a couch, their hands and feet tied tightly with rope. They wore zombie masks displaying expressions of fear and astonishment.

Two more Play Things stood over them, one holding a fake crossbow aimed at the couch and the other clutching a glass beaker of black goo labeled *"CRUDE OIL."* These two Play Things wore masks that were slightly different from those of the couch zombies.

The crossbow zombie wore a mask that bore the wise, kind expression of my mom, while the oil-clutching zombie wore a mask featuring the evil sneer, sharp cheekbones, and pointy chin of a certain not-so-dear aunt of mine.

All of the actors on stage wore the tropical zombie outfits from the rehearsal a few nights ago. All the actors, that is, except the fake aunt. She wore a black turtleneck, round sunglasses, a large wireless earpiece, and a white, fluffy wig.

"What does this all mean?" Nerida whispered.

"It means mischief," I told her with a wicked smile. "The kind of mischief that could save Deadmark."

"Listen up!" said the fake mom holding the fake crossbow. "One of you is secretly destroying the lab's renewable energy. The solar panels are smashed, the wind turbines are busted, and the bone compost biofuel converter is completely missing."

The tied-up zombies gasped and gulped. "What's even

worse," said the fake mom, "is that we've found drops of crude oil all over the laboratory. Show them, sister!"

The fake aunt held the beaker of oil before the face of each zombie on the couch. They all recoiled in disgust as she walked it past them.

"One of you is dripping in oil and destroying our renewable energy," continued the fake mom. "Which means one of you is not who you seem. But we can't tell which one of you it is, because somehow you're blending in with the rest of us."

"Get me off of this couch!" cried one of the tied-up zombies as she struggled against the ropes. "I love science, I promise! I can't get enough of it!"

"Silence!" cried the fake mom. "I'm the Lead Scientist at this research facility, so I'm in charge. Before we untie anyone, we're going to find out who is anti-science and who isn't."

The fake mom turned to face the audience. "I know I'm a zombie with good intentions," she said. She was staring straight at Agonista. "However, one of you pretends to be a zombie with good intentions, but is actually the complete opposite. One of you is here with evil goals, and we're going to find out who you are."

Hearing the cue, a Play Thing wearing a troll mask turned a soft spotlight on Agonista from above the stage. She was now a part of this play, whether she liked it or not.

"Oooh, look at Agonista squirm!" I whispered to Bram. I watched with delight as my (real) aunt slunk even lower in her seat, crossed her arms, uncrossed them, and coughed nervously into her fist.

On stage, the fake mom turned back to the tied-up zombies. She used one hand to keep the crossbow aimed at the couch while her other hand pulled a $20 Ignorwegian bill from her pocket.

"The only reason you'd be interested in fossil fuels is to collect Ignorwegian money," she said. "Now, I'm going to light this $20 bill on fire. The greedy, anti-science fiend among us won't be able to take it, and they'll lose control. Then we'll know who you are."

"Sister, wait," urged the fake aunt. The Play Thing performing the fake-aunt role did an excellent job imitating Agonista's distinct, crackly voice. "Before we do anything hasty, let's have a drink of brain fluid to cool off. It sure is hot in here, right?"

"What do you think is going to happen?" I whispered to Nerida with a smirk.

"I don't know," she said. "But that lady's protests sure seem suspicious."

The fake aunt set the beaker of oil down on a table, staggered over to the refrigerator at the front of the stage, and took out a glass bottle of brain fluid.

Then, with her back to the other zombies on stage, she pulled from her pocket a bottle filled with pink sparkly goo—another excellent prop courtesy of the Play Things. She held it before the audience and stage whispered so we all could hear: "Shh. This is humanizer mutagen. One sip will turn my sister into a ghastly human!" She then gave us a secretive thumbs-up gesture.

Everyone in the theater gasped in unison. Then, after a beat, they began to holler and boo. Some threw handfuls of popbrain toward the stage.

Nerida grabbed me by my shoulders. "Edda—what are you implying?" she whispered harshly.

"Shh," I said, pointing to the stage. "Just wait and see."

The fake aunt poured the mutagen into the bottle of brain fluid and swirled it around. She walked over to the fake mom and held the drink before her.

"My sister, you're the Lead Scientist of this research lab," said the fake aunt as she snagged the $20 bill out of the fake mom's hand. "So, naturally, you should have the first sip."

"OK, sis," said the fake mom. "That seems reasonable. Plus, I trust you since you're my sister. It would be unthinkable for you to steer me wrong or betray me. I'll take a sip."

The fake mom set down her prop crossbow and slowly— agonizingly slowly—lifted the glass to her face.

As soon as the liquid touched the mouth of her mask, smoke erupted on stage and the fake mom fell to the ground, writhing in convincing agony. The audience gasped again.

The fake aunt howled in celebration while the fake mom moaned and twisted on the ground. Though I helped write it, even I cringed a little at the realistic scene.

"Hahahaha!" cried the fake aunt, turning toward the audience. "Now that my sister is a human, I will become the Lead Scientist! And all the oil beneath Fallapartica will be mine!"

The real Agonista was in her balcony screeching orders to Cabbagio, Squeak, and Gibber. Her guilt was so apparent, it may as well have been wafting up from her head like steam. She looked completely trapped.

The fake mom slowly rose to her feet with a spotlight illuminating her new, horrid human appearance. The special effects team had done an amazing job creating a dreadfully smooth-skinned human mask topped by a curly brown wig. The mask now featured vivid green eyes peering out across the audience with shocking intensity.

The zombies tied to the couch struggled against their ropes. "BRRRAAAINS!" they cried feverishly. "BRAAAINS!"

I tittered with excitement as black, sticky goo began oozing from the fake aunt's wig, gushing over her face and onto the floor. The Play Things had pulled off the stage trick flawlessly.

"You fools never stood a chance," she crowed as the black sludge began spurting out of her sleeves. The fake oil was coming down from her wig with such force, it was difficult to understand her garbled words. "Now your country is mine!"

Completely silent, the zombies in the audience gawked at the spectacle before them.

I, on other hand, was in a fit of laughter. But my eyes weren't on the play. They were trained on Agonista in her balcony. Shiny beads of sweat glistened in the spotlight as they ran down her face. It almost looked like her face was melting.

"Turn on the lights!" she cried, standing up with her arms spread wide above her head. "Everyone out! This play is over!"

My smile blazed toward the balcony as Agonista stood trapped in the spotlight's exposing beam. I knew now, without the tiniest shred of doubt, that she had humanized my mom. The human in the coal mine was telling the truth. That human was my mom.

And there was my aunt, in all her wickedness, guilty and embarrassed for all the world to see.

CHAPTER NINE
OUTRAGEOUS FORTUNE

Stunned zombies staggered toward the exits. This was more drama than they had bargained for. They murmured and bumped into each other as they glanced up at Agonista, who still loomed in her balcony, dabbing her forehead with a cloth.

Gibber harnessed Squeak, jumped down from the balcony, and bounded onto the stage. They stalked to the backstage area on the hunt for Rick and the Play Things. But, just as we planned, the dramatists had already retreated into the secret chamber beneath the stage.

Agonista's sunglasses-covered eyes zipped around the pit. When she located me, it was as if a rope of ice connected us across the theater.

I stood up and clapped loudly. "Bravo! Bravo! Encore!" I stuck my fingers in my mouth and attempted a whistle, but all that came out was a high-pitched sputter.

My aunt screeched with rage and disappeared through the side exit of her balcony and into the lobby. Cabbagio followed closely behind.

The final audience member exited the pit, leaving Bram, Nerida, and I as the only ones left. Nerida looked panicked by the real-world suggestions of the play.

"Edda, how much of that play is real?" Nerida stared at me pleadingly with wild, bloodshot eyes. "Are you accusing Agonista of humanizing your mom? Did she steal the mutagen we created? Or did she make it herself? Why won't you tell me what's going on?"

"Ha! Maybe because you hate me?" I replied, spinning away from her.

"No, I don't—and you know it!" she snapped. "If anything, you hate me!"

"Edda, Nerida," Bram said quickly. "Cabbagio's here."

Nerida and I turned to face the pit's entrance. Cabbagio walked toward us, his flaky bald head gleaming in the lights above.

"You have greatly offended your aunt, Edda," he said. As he approached us, he fiddled nervously with the gem around his neck. "It's bad luck to disturb your elders."

"My elders?" I exclaimed. "What's more offensive—a play put on by children, or my elders actually destroying Deadmark with anti-science nonsense?"

"What if Edda's right, Dad?" asked Nerida, stepping toward him. "What if Agonista really is taking Deadmark down a path of ruin?"

Cabbagio laughed. "You kids think you know everything, but you have so much to learn. The best we can do is to rally behind our new leader instead of criticizing her constantly. Complaining doesn't get us anywhere."

"Rally behind our new leader?" I spat, clutching a handful of my hair. "The same leader who humanized my mom so she could take over Deadmark?"

Nerida looked stunned. "Oh no," she said, looking at me with enormous eyes, her hand covering her mouth. "Your mom really was humanized. I'm so sorry, Edda."

Nerida took another step toward her father. "Please, Dad. Edda is telling the truth."

"You have to believe her," said Bram. "I saw Edda's mom with my own eyes—she's a human in Ignorway, and this play proved that Agonista's responsible."

Cabbagio looked at me without a trace of emotion. "I'm sorry, but my intuition tells me that Agonista would never do something like that. And intuition is my strong suit." Then, with a shrug, he added: "I don't believe you."

All the positive, victorious post-play feelings had vanished. I realized then that even if I had proven Agonista's guilt, it probably wouldn't matter anyway. Not with zombies like Cabbagio in positions of power.

Agonista had already deceived and bribed, spoiled and stuffed Cabbagio and the Elected Council to the point where they would never turn against her. They were all on her side. Why would they believe a kid like me if it meant giving up their endless rewards for staying silent?

Something in me snapped, and I climbed up on stage.

"Hear that, Nerida?" I asked, looking down at her, Bram, and Cabbagio. "He doesn't believe me, and the Elected Council won't either. That's what I was saying earlier—Deadmark is doomed. We might as well crawl back into the cemetery. Zombies crept out of Ignorwegian graves for nothing."

"Please stop saying that!" said Nerida. "We have to keep fighting!"

"Agonista has the Elected Council and your dad wrapped around her finger," I said. "And they're taking us all down with them."

"Giving up can't be the answer!" said Bram. "No matter how bad it gets."

"You're both wrong," I said. I pulled the actual humanizer mutagen out of my pocket and clutched it in my hand.

"Is that real!?" asked Nerida, her hands in her hair. "Please tell me that's a prop."

"She's really lost it!" cried Cabbagio. He clutched his gem in fear.

"We've all lost it!" I yelled. "We've lost everything Deadmark was founded on. We might as well all be humans. Agonista is guilty of turning my mom into a human, but there will be no justice. With my aunt in charge, science has no future. We have no future. *I* have no future."

Like I was wielding a dagger, I waved and stabbed the air with the jar of mutagen. "Maybe I should just splash this on Agonista and turn her into a human. An eye for an eye!"

"You can't threaten the Lead Scientist like that!" Cabbagio cried indignantly. "It's…it's…inappropriate!"

"Edda, please come down from there," said Bram. "Humanizing Agonista, or any zombie, is not the answer. All that will do is create one more misguided human, which is the last thing the world needs."

"Bram's right," said Nerida. "Things aren't great right now, but that doesn't mean your future is ruined."

Deep down, I knew my friends were right. Yet I still wondered how we could come back from this. My mom was a human, Deadmark was falling apart, and Agonista was getting away with betraying our country.

Still, as I looked at the faces of my friends, I couldn't help but feel a slight pang of hope. With friends like these, the future had to be at least a little positive.

As I stepped toward the edge of the stage to hop down, I heard a noise behind me. Then Bram shouted: "Edda! Look out!"

I whipped around to see Squeak and Gibber lurching toward me from the backstage area. Panicked, I turned to get down from the stage. I didn't look where I was stepping, and my foot slipped on a puddle of fake oil from the play.

I yelped as I tumbled face first into the pit, using both hands to break my fall. I heard the sound of shattering glass followed by Nerida screaming, "Dad!" Then I heard a dreadful sound that I'll never forget for the rest of my death: It was Cabbagio, wailing in agony.

Sprawled out on my stomach, my face was smashed into

the popbrain-littered floor. I lifted my aching head to see Cabbagio's bare feet right before my eyes. They were fizzing, steaming, full of sparkles.

My eyes widened in disbelief. The shock might have killed me if I wasn't already dead. As I fell off the stage, I must have dropped the bottle of mutagen. It had broken on the floor and splashed all over Cabbagio's exposed feet.

I stood up and checked myself—incredibly, none of the mutagen had touched my skin.

As I backed away in terror, Cabbagio screamed and writhed on the ground. His flaky skin was smoothing out like magic as flurries of colorful sparkles glittered across his face, hands, and feet.

"Oh, I've been humanized!" he wailed as his eyeballs grew whiter and a plump human nose sprouted from his face. He began rubbing his gemstone rings all over his body in an attempt to counteract the mutagen. It didn't work.

"My body!" he yelled. "The Power Gems do nothing!"

"Dad, no!" cried Nerida. "You have to get out of here! We'll eat your brain!"

Nerida turned to Bram and grabbed his hoodie with both hands, pulling him toward her. "Zombies can't control themselves, but maybe a vampire can. Get him to the Undead Sea and onto the first human ship you find. It's his only chance!"

"No problem—I had a big lunch," said Bram. He let out a shrill whistle and yelled, "Yo, Rick! Let's go!"

Rick came whooshing out from beneath the stage. With Rick leading the way, Bram helped the wailing Cabbagio to his feet and rushed him to the exit.

Momentarily stunned, Gibber jumped down from the stage with Squeak on his back. He carefully tiptoed his bare feet around the fizzing puddle and lumbered after the humanized Cabbagio.

"Leave them!" yelled Agonista as she burst into the pit. "We have what we need right here."

Nerida's sobs filled my head. Frozen in shock, I just stood there staring at the pink, sparkly puddle as Agonista closed in on me.

Squeak and Gibber hurried to Agonista's side. She snapped at them in a whisper I could just barely make out: "You fools said there was only one bottle of mutagen!"

Gibber mumbled in apologetic tones, and Squeak said, "Sorry, ma'am. We heard her coming up the steps and had to get out of there in a hurry…"

"Forget it," she said as they boxed me in. "All's well that ends well, I suppose."

Agonista placed a bony hand on my shoulder. "Edda, you are hereby detained for the brash crime of humanization." She wore the grin of a hostile jack-o'-lantern. "And here I thought I'd have to invent a reason to throw you into the dungeon."

Squeak pulled a chain out of his harness and handed it to Gibber. As Gibber wrapped it around my wrists, I felt my last remaining shreds of hope shrivel up and blow away like so many particles of meaningless dust.

CHAPTER TEN

THE QUICK AND THE DEAD

here was one good thing about being tossed into a dungeon: It gave me plenty of time to ponder my situation. And I had a lot to ponder.

I felt as though I had experienced emotional whiplash. In just a few minutes, I had swung harshly from the thrilling highs of a successful play to the deep disgrace of an accidental humanization.

But there were no ups and downs in the dungeons beneath Zømborg Castle. Here, there was only down.

And here, in the middle of the day, surrounded by cold, inky stone, my thoughts were as dark as my surroundings.

With my elbows propped on my knees and both fists

clutching handfuls of hair, I sat inside the slight depression that served as their poor excuse for a grave. There wasn't so much as a shovelful of dirt to make it somewhat comfortable.

I had been locked up for several hours, but it felt like weeks.

"Gah!" I moaned into the darkness. "That it should come to this!" I didn't care if Squeak and Gibber heard me. I knew they were stationed outside because now and then their muffled bickering came through the thin opening beneath the steel cell door.

Even with their noises and my own groaning, I could have sworn I heard other sorrowful sounds vibrating up and around the stone walls of my cell. It sounded like moaning. Once again, I was compelled to question my grasp of reality.

Those mournful sounds couldn't be real. To my knowledge, Zømborg's underground dungeons hadn't held prisoners for decades. Until me, that is.

Without easy answers, I tried my best to block it out. I had plenty of other worries to focus on besides dungeon ghosts.

I picked at the tray of freeze-dried brain chips they had given me. It was the barest minimum nutrition to keep me from starving.

As bad as I felt for Cabbagio, I felt worse for Nerida and Argo. No one deserves a humanized dad. Apparently, I had a knack for finding new ways to bring Nerida heartache.

There was one shred of hope in all this, and it hinged on whether Bram and Rick could guide Cabbagio to safety before zombies ate his brain. Even if he'd always be human, at least Nerida and Argo would still have a dad. Sort of.

In between bouts of sorrow for Nerida and her family, I had plenty of time to feel sorry for myself.

"It feels like everyone's against me," I sneered, tossing the brain chips into the corner. "A braver zombie would have just humanized Agonista and been done with it. But I'm not brave. I just put on plays and humanize zombies by mistake."

A little cockroach skittered beneath the steel door and into my cell. With antennae quickly flitting up and down, it chirped and darted toward the brain chips scattered in the corner.

I crawled over to watch the cockroach enjoy its snack. "What is the point of all this?" I asked the insect, which, as a cockroach, couldn't respond. "I'm supposed to just eat and sleep in my cell, and then what? I'm no better or more important than you…um, no offense."

Then, like a waking daymare, as if the universe were proving that things could always, always get worse, a head-sized slat opened in the cell door. The dim light revealed Agonista's long, skeletal face. I instinctively hugged my knees into my body for protection.

From behind the door slat, my aunt's sunglasses pointed

at the cockroach munching on the brain chips. It was beyond me how she could see through the darkness while wearing sunglasses.

"Making friends, I see?" she asked with a smirk.

Between the interference from the metal door and the crackling from her earpiece, it sounded like I was talking to a demonic robot.

"That cockroach has more integrity in one antenna than you have in your entire body," I said. She smiled, seeming to take my insult as a compliment. This zombie had no shame.

"Well, it isn't integrity that's stopping me from humanizing you on the spot, like I did your mom," she said, her smile growing wider. "And even if I had more mutagen, I wouldn't waste it on you. No, after that little performance, I have a different, far messier fate in store for my niece."

I stood up, fists clenched, my eyes narrowed into slits. Hearing Agonista admit to my mom's humanization shook something loose inside of me. "Why are you doing this? You've betrayed your family, your entire country, for what?"

"You're too young to understand," she said condescendingly. "Someday you'll get your priorities straight. Believe it or not, I do feel a little bad that Squeak and Gibber ate your mom's brain and tossed her into the sea. I did love her...to an extent. The truth is, I just love being rich a whole lot more."

Clenching my jaw, I tried hard to conceal my shock. *Agonista thinks Squeak and Gibber ate my mom's brain...she has no idea my mom escaped?*

Just then, the moaning sound wandered into my cell once again.

A sinister grin flashed on Agonista's face. "Ah, you forgot to mention the Elected Council. I betrayed them, too. They were gullible and so easily distracted by fancy brains, but they started to catch wind of what I was up to. It's much easier to just lock them up. Strategic betrayals have always been key to my success in business."

This was so many levels beyond outrageous. "What makes you think you can get away with this? What makes you think you're more important than everyone else in Deadmark?"

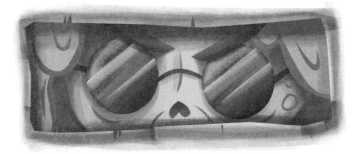

Agonista shrugged. "The climate is ruined. Why not make some money off it? That dead dinosaur goo beneath Deadmark is much more valuable than kidding ourselves into believing we can use science to find a way off this sinking ship. Wrecking all of Deadmark's sustainable technology is just the beginning of my plan to sidestep the ReConstitution and fully transition Deadmark to fossil fuels."

"Zombies won't stand for it," I sneered. "Eventually, they'll learn what you're doing and Deadmark will fight back."

"Aww," she cooed with disdain. "You're so adorably naïve. Zombies are already falling in line. Anti-science ideas are spreading across Deadmark like wildfire. And all it took was the spark of a few well-placed rumors. Believe me, niece—it's only going to get worse."

"You're a monster," I said, "the bad kind." I took a step toward her and glared with all the strength I could muster. "You might as well be human."

Agonista's shrill, tinny laughter erupted with a high-pitched force that made me cringe. I plugged my ears as it echoed painfully off the walls of my cell. The cockroach skittered defensively into the corner.

"Yeah, well, we're all going to end up in the same place anyway," she said, struggling to catch her breath. "Zombies, humans…" she pointed to the cockroach, which crouched even lower at the unwanted attention, "…even cockroaches."

Without the slightest hint of emotion, she sighed and said, "When the climate collapses, we're all going to collapse along with it."

Of all the terrible things my aunt had said, these words hit me the hardest. She was echoing the same misguided logic I had preached to Nerida back in her lab.

How could I allow myself to adopt the same conclusions as my aunt? How could I give up on science and stop fighting to save my country? To save the world?

I swore to myself that from then on, I wouldn't let my negative thoughts get in the way of fighting for what was right. Somehow, someway, I was going to get my revenge on Agonista...and save Deadmark from ruin.

"So, anyway," she said. "I'm sending you to Fangland to join the werewolves for dinner, if you catch my drift. I've done a lot of business with those dogs over the years, and they owe me a favor. They're quite obedient—I know they won't howl about it to anyone."

I wasn't going to let Agonista scare me. With a deep breath, I let peals of laughter take over my body. They rolled through me like ferocious thunder. Agonista's clear discomfort made me laugh even harder.

She snorted, and her face moved away from the door slat. Before she walked away, I heard her bark: "Squeak, Gibber! Tonight you're going to take this criminal to your ship and sail her to Fangland. Don't draw attention to yourselves by taking a fleet—just take the one ship."

I heard a rustle of paper. "Oh, and the werewolves don't have email," she said. "So give them this envelope when you arrive—they'll know exactly how to deal with her."

After chaining my hands and feet, Squeak and Gibber marched me through the moldy underground tunnels beneath the castle. Drips echoed around us as we trudged through fusty thresholds and up and down musty stone steps.

At certain points, I could hear echoes of the Elected Council's moans rising up from somewhere deep in the caverns.

"That evil witch sure has you brainwashed, doesn't she?" I asked in a mocking tone. Gibber pushed me forward with a baseball bat. "I mean, how could you let her imprison the Elected Council? Whatever happened to democracy? Surely you're aware of the concept."

Gibber shrugged. Squeak scoffed from atop Gibber's shoulders.

"You're going to regret this," I said. "Democracy protects everyone, even dunderheads like you. Without the Elected Council, Agonista will do whatever she wants, and eventually she'll turn on you. And there will be no one to stop her."

"She's the Lead Scientist," said Squeak, with a sneer. "She can do what she wants."

Gibber moaned unintelligibly.

"Aye," said Squeak. "Gibber's right. If Agonista's not happy, Deadmark's not happy."

"That's not how that works," I snapped. "Thoughtless words are worse than no words at all."

We exited the tunnel, and the wind slammed into my body. The gust pulled my hair back and dried out my already dehydrated eyeballs. The chains prevented me from protecting my face.

I struggled to open my eyes against the wind. Eventually I saw that we were outside of the Zømborg Castle grounds, just southeast of the Circle of Willis. Gibber's jabs guided me down the stone path and toward the dockyards of East Ganglia Bay.

"Is there anything you spongeheads wouldn't do for her?" I asked, cringing as I leaned into the wind. "Has it occurred to you that you're taking me to get devoured by werewolves? Why else would you sail me to Fangland?"

"What's your problem, anyway?" asked Squeak. "You could have been one of your aunt's top advisors. Running your mouth isn't helping anyone."

"*Running my mouth*?!" I snapped. "Your so-called Lead Scientist admitted to humanizing my mom and selling out our country for oil money. As citizens of Deadmark, running our mouths is the least we should be doing."

"Agonista is our leader now," said Squeak, sounding like a programmed android. "If she thinks fossil fuels are best, then so be it."

Gibber moaned in agreement. These two were beyond help. It felt like a virus of indifference had infected zombiekind.

I struggled against my chains, and Gibber rudely ushered me toward the docks. As we approached, dozens of ships came into view, listing and swaying in the stormy seas. Some were for brain hunting, some for commerce, and others for scientific research.

Sailor zombies hurried past in a bustle of activity. They rolled barrels, carried cords of rope, and pushed supply-filled wheelbarrows.

Two astronomer zombies walked past hauling a special telescope called a smogoscope. It's used to observe stars and planets beyond the thick layer of pollution choking our atmosphere. I seized the opportunity.

"Help! Fellow scientists! Help!" I screamed. "They're taking me to Fangland to be devoured by werewolves!"

With pained expressions, the astronomers just kept walking. I heard a ruffling sound behind my head, and then I felt cloth material wrap tightly around my mouth. I cried out in protest,

but all that came out was a muffled grumble.

"That's just about enough of that, isn't it?" Squeak asked rhetorically.

My mind grasped frantically at wild, semi-realistic schemes to get out of this predicament, but we had already reached our destination: a three-masted ship called *The Quick and the Dead*. It was Squeak and Gibber's ship—the largest brain-hunting vessel in all of Deadmark.

Massive and wooden, *The Quick and the Dead* was a relic from a bygone era. Zombies had seized it from Ignorwegians when they emigrated from Ignorway more than 100 years ago. Not only was it a symbol of zombie dominance, it also served as the most productive and fearsome brain-hunting ship on the sea.

Despite its enormous size, the powerful stormy seas rocked *The Quick and the Dead* like a cradle. Large gray sails rippled and billowed in the wind, each of them adorned with the emblem of the Deadmark flag: a brain with atomic swirls orbiting around it.

The sailor zombies were more numerous now. They scurried along the docks and toiled aboard the ship, tightening masts, stocking weapons, coiling rope, scrubbing decks, and taking care of all the finishing touches to ready the ship for the open seas.

Under very different circumstances, I might have admired their industriousness.

Squeak's prodding led me up the gangway and onto their ship. Sailors briefly paused their chores to salute their captains as we passed. Some of them eyed me with hints of empathy, but fear of their commanders outweighed all other emotions.

Gibber pulled my chains toward a waist-high iron ring screwed into the deck at the very back of the ship.

I now faced the sea with the rest of the ship behind me. Gibber looped my chains through the ring and tightened until there was no wiggle room. I felt a tug on my ankle chains as if to make sure they were tight, and then someone ripped the gag away from my mouth.

"Scream at the water, for all we care," said Squeak with a chuckle. "There are no fishies left in it to hear you."

I heard them walk away as their buffoonish laughter mixed with my cries of protest. All the sounds drifted senselessly upward before dissolving in the toxic sea air.

Days passed, maybe even weeks. On the open water, the sea and wind raged as if trying to determine which was stronger.

The incessant fog, the slashing acid rain, and the ship's rollercoaster swings combined to wear down my consciousness. At times I wasn't sure if I was awake and hallucinating, or asleep and dreaming. Either way, it all seemed wrong and surreal.

Green vapors rose up from the sea as the fog unfurled around us like a puffy, poisonous blanket.

I couldn't see more than a dozen feet in front of my face. The few ship lights I could see barely illuminated the fog immediately surrounding them, leaving glowing orbs in the haze like little half-alive pixies.

Every once in a while—not nearly often enough—a stale, salty brain cake would slip onto the bannister in front of me. I never saw who put it there. Perhaps it was a good Samaritan sailor or a fan of my mom's, or perhaps Squeak and Gibber just wanted me to stay healthy enough to remain appetizing for the werewolves.

Either way, every time, I would lean my head down to eagerly gobble it up before it slid off into the sea.

At a certain point, visions began to appear in the darkness. I could see Nerida at the bottom of her undersea lab without a helmet, her face in her hands, sobbing. Then there was my mom, a transparent, glowing human wandering the castle ramparts, like a fairy-tale ghost, calling to me from the beyond.

I closed my eyes tight and shook my head to make the visions disappear. I must have lost consciousness, because the next thing I remember was a panicked siren blaring across the ship. White lights switched over to flashing red alarms that reflected off the thinning fog in front of me. Despite the noise, I could hear zombie sailors scampering about.

From somewhere above, a megaphoned voice blared: "Code gray! Code gray! Ignorwegian ships off the port stern! To the battle stations! We have a human fleet coming in for attack!"

CHAPTER ELEVEN
SLINGS AND ARROWS

I felt helpless as zombie sailors shouted and scurried outside of my vision.

The Quick and the Dead dipped and swayed violently in the crashing sea. When the ship dunked downward over a rolling wave, I could see the masts of steel warships streaking toward us like swarming sea phantoms.

Was this another hallucination? Was I dreaming?

My visibility across the sea wasn't great, but the fog surrounding the ship had noticeably receded. Atop the steel masts, Ignorwegian flags flapped madly in the wind. Their flag was a white banner with Ignorway's red national emblem: an ostrich with its head in the sand. Ironically, ostriches have been extinct in Ignorway for more than a century.

As *The Quick and the Dead* pitched upward on a wave, the approaching ships would disappear from view. And each time we dipped back downward, the Ignorwegian fleet was much closer than before.

I swung my head side to side to get the splashing rain out of my eyes. But there wasn't much I could do without the use of my hands. The ship dunked downward again, and I blinked furiously to clear my vision.

Barely visible through the haze, I caught sight of several humans peering over the bow of the lead vessel. They were easy to identify by their customary Ignorwegian tinfoil hats glistening beneath the lights of their ship.

Among the humans in the lead ship, I saw a streak of blue light.

I squinted hard to make it out, but *The Quick and the Dead* flung upward, and the lead human ship left my sight.

When *The Quick and the Dead* dropped down again, I could see the approaching sailors in detail. Some were in raincoats, and others wore heavy long-sleeve shirts made of synthetic material. They were armed with zombie-hunting weapons like slingshots, crossbows, machetes, axes, and baseball bats. From this distance, they appeared to be tidier, less decomposed versions of the zombie sailors on my ship.

I had never seen a human in the flesh before...that is, before I watched Cabbagio transform into a human before my eyes. Now there were shiploads of them rocketing toward me.

Then, for the first time in a long while, a smile covered my face: There beside the humans was a floating blue skull and a fluttering bat.

Was this actually happening? "Please be real, please be real, please be real..." I repeated into the wind.

When *The Quick and the Dead* plunged downward again, the human ships had disappeared from my view. Perhaps they were circling around to find a point of entry.

While I couldn't see the panicked commotion taking place behind my back, I sure could hear it. It was frighteningly loud, and my inability to defend myself made it all the more nerve-racking.

With all my might, I tried to yank myself free of the chains. They wouldn't budge. I screamed out in frustration into the deafening wind. There was nothing I could do but stand there, chained to the ship, waiting for things to play out.

BOOM! BOOM! BOOM! BOOM! The Quick and the Dead's skull cannons blasted in rapid succession, causing tremors to course through the floorboards beneath my feet.

Zombie sailors cursed at the humans, at each other, and at their bad luck. "How did these humans know we were going to Fangland?!" yelled a sailor. "We *never* go to Fangland!"

Colorful flares lit up the skies around me in bright blasts of red, purple, and green. It was like witnessing a very dramatic, very dangerous fireworks display.

PING! PING! PING! Slingshot balls caromed off the hull of the ship, followed by the *THUNK! THUNK! THUNK!* of arrows. If the humans were close enough to land slings and arrows, were they also boarding the ship? Were they already aboard?

Screams, slams, and battle cries filled the air. Without being able to see anything behind me, I couldn't tell if I was hearing the yells of zombies or humans.

Then I heard a frenzied voice. It didn't sound like a zombie. "Ha! I got one over here," said the voice, approaching my back. "Looks like the prisoner they mentioned."

My spine stiffened as something poked my back. It felt like a large stick, perhaps a baseball bat. Suddenly, my mouth began watering at the overwhelming smell of human brains. My nose had confirmed it: It was a human.

This is where the curtain drops on the tragedy of Edda, I thought. *Slain while hungry.*

I tried growling and groaning and whipping my head from side to side to scare the human away, but this type of human was not easily scared by zombies. It just laughed.

"Hey! Knock it off!" a familiar voice called out behind me. The weapon left my back. "We had one rule," said the voice, approaching, "no hurting anyone, especially the prisoner. You humans aren't the best listeners, are you?"

"Whatever, bloodsucker," snarled the human. I could hear his footsteps squeak on the sea-soaked wooden deck as he walked away.

Bram's bright vampire smile filled my vision. He was leaning around in front of me so I could see his face. He then showed me a large pair of bolt cutters.

"Hey, Edda," he said in a casual tone. "Anything new?"

I rolled my eyes and Bram groaned with effort as he squeezed the bolt cutters into my chains.

It had been a while since I'd had a non-imagined conversation, so my attempt at a full sentence sputtered out in bursts. "How…? Humans…? What…?"

Before Bram could respond, a friendly blue light came swooping in.

"Hey, Edda! Good to see you again," said Rick as he floated his forehead into mine for a gentle head-bump greeting. "We have all the zombie sailors rounded up. I can't believe our plan is actually working. Improvisation can be a thrill."

Bram gave the chains one final clip, and they fell to my feet. Rubbing my wrists, I turned around.

On the ship's deck, about two dozen armed human sailors in tinfoil hats surrounded the zombie sailors. From the zombies' moans and shouts, I could tell they were divided evenly between furious anger and voracious hunger for the human brains surrounding them.

Squeak and Gibber stood in the middle of the zombie group. Their eyes were fixed on me, their faces warped with rage. I responded with a smile and shrug.

On all sides of *The Quick and the Dead*, Ignorwegian vessels bobbed and swayed. Human eyes glowered from their ships, their contempt for zombies unmistakable. Many of them sucked irritably on plastic cups, likely filled with the Choke-branded mush my mom had mentioned.

Despite the surreal situation unfolding around me, all I could think about was the intense, enticing smell of brains. I shook my head, digging deep into my reserves of willpower to block out the aromas invading my nostrils.

Bram must have noticed me sniffing the air and drooling a little.

"Here," he said, handing me a stick of brain-block. "I grabbed this before we left Deadmark. Thought it might come in handy."

I applied the balm under my nostrils. Apparently Bram had picked up the cinnamon-scented variety. It wasn't perfect, but, with concentration, it did the trick.

"So," I said with a deep inhalation of artificial cinnamon scent. "How is this happening? How did you find me?"

"Rick and I helped Cabbagio escape," said Bram. "We borrowed a boat and sailed him out to the first human ship we could find. It was a drill ship looking for oil wells beneath the sea."

A zombie tried to grab a human, and the human jabbed him with a baseball bat. "Hey! Easy there!" yelled Rick.

"When we got back to Deadmark," Bram continued, "everyone was talking about the Elected Council banishing you to Fangland for your crime."

"Agonista is lying!" I shouted. "She banished me herself without even consulting the Elected Council—the same Elected Council she has locked up in the dungeons, by the way!"

"Wow," said Bram, shaking his head. "She's growing more corrupt by the minute."

From a nearby Ignorwegian ship, one of the humans yelled, "Hey, creeps! How's my brain smell?" Squeak yelled back,

"Creeps? You're the ones wearing tinfoil and slurping down plastic!"

"We learned from some zombie sailors that Squeak and Gibber had left without their usual armada protecting them," said Rick. "We figured a human fleet could overtake a single zombie ship—even if that ship happened to be *The Quick and The Dead*."

"So we flew out to sea to find a zombie-hunting ship," said Bram. "We found these humans and made a deal with the captain to help us rescue you. He was so afraid of Squeak and Gibber that he wasn't very open to the idea at first..." Bram scratched his head sheepishly. "So I may have tried to hypnotize him a little. But I think I just ended up giving us both headaches."

Bram nodded toward a human wearing a peacoat and a tinfoil hat that was much larger than the other sailors'. He was seated on a barrel with his head in his hands.

"I used everything we learned in Mrs. Caligari's hypnotic arts class, but no luck," said Bram.

"It was a really good try," said Rick. "You'll get the hang of it eventually."

"So, as a last-ditch bargaining effort," Bram said with a grimace, "I kinda promised the humans they could keep *The Quick and The Dead*...I hope you don't mind."

While the thought of *The Quick and the Dead* falling into Ignorwegian hands filled me with disgust, it was a far better option than being devoured by werewolves in Fangland.

"N-no, I, uh, think that's a fair trade, all things considered," I said. "I mean, I can't thank you guys enough for saving me. I'm not exactly in a position to nitpick."

Rick nodded. "OK, you heard her," he called to the humans. "Get those zombies onto deathboats. Then the ship is yours. Gentle now!"

"You're a traitor, Edda!" cried Squeak, as he, Gibber, and the rest of the zombies were forced onto deathboats—the small aluminum boats that hung from the ship in case of emergencies. I wanted to yell out, "*No, you are!*" but that seemed a little petty, given the circumstances.

With yells, prods, and pokes from the humans, the zombies eventually obeyed. Apparently, their desire to avoid being speared with sharp arrows or whacked by baseball bats won out over their desire to feast on human brains.

"As soon as the zombies start rowing back to Deadmark, we're going to get in our own deathboat," said Bram. "We'll take the one with a motor, so the zombies can't catch us and get revenge. Maybe we can go to Gormany and hide out for a while until things simmer down."

I knew that Agonista wouldn't hesitate to arrest me again if we made our way back to Deadmark. But that's where Nerida was, and I couldn't just abandon her after what I had done.

"Thank you both so much for saving Nerida's dad," I said. "She must have been thrilled when you gave her the news."

Bram didn't respond. He just stared at me and blinked.

"Bram," I said. "You were able to let her know that you saved Cabbagio, weren't you?"

Bram's face darkened. He bowed his head.

I placed my hand on his shoulder. "What is it?"

"I'm so sorry, Edda," he said, avoiding my eyes.

Rick floated close to me, tears welling around his sockets.

"Edda," he said. "We got to her lab, but she wasn't there. The lab was trashed. There was an empty bottle labeled "*HUMANIZER*" on a table, a pile of human outfits on the floor, and a trail of cheese puffs leading down her tower steps to the sea. Her boat was gone."

"Wait—what are you saying?" I asked, shaking my head in disbelief.

"I'm so sorry, Edda," Bram repeated. "Nerida must have been so upset about her dad being humanized that she...she humanized herself and took off to join him in Ignorway."

CHAPTER TWELVE

AN ARMY OF SORROWS

The fuming, toxic waves were never-ending. With the motor off, the small deathboat lurched and seesawed in the middle of the Undead Sea.

Bram had his feet stretched on the seat in front of him. Rick floated by my side, his skull slowly rotating as he puzzled through our situation.

After motoring away from the humans and the zombies, I asked Bram to kill the engine. While I appreciated his idea to hide out in Gormany, I wasn't quite ready to commit to it.

We had some time to spare before Squeak and Gibber's motorless deathboat would catch up to us. So for now, we just floated aimlessly and considered our options.

Thanks to my actions, none of them were great.

With Nerida gone, my desire to return to Deadmark had dropped considerably. Was it worth risking another visit to the dungeons—or worse? And for how long could I hide in Gormany? I couldn't just move there and change my name. Could I?

No matter which option I chose, the outlook felt bleak. Back in the dungeon, I had promised myself I wouldn't let my negative emotions get the best of me, but the fact that Nerida was a human—and it was my fault—made that promise pretty much impossible to keep.

Nerida was always so poised and logical. Humanizing herself in a fit of despair seemed out of character, but I knew as well as anyone the ways that grief could warp the mind and cause strange behavior. Her broken heart must have taken over her mind.

It pained me to consider that she had come to the Glob to make up with me. She wanted to be my friend again. And then...I humanized her dad and ruined it all.

How much sadness was I supposed to handle? It really seemed that when sorrows came, it was never just one at a time. It was a whole army of them at once.

"Edda, you're gnashing again," said Bram. He pulled a plastic container from his backpack. With a frown, he took off the lid and removed a big, juicy brain. He handed it to me and quickly wiped his fingers on his hoodie sleeve. "You must be starving. I snagged this from the ship before we took off."

"Thanks," I said, eying the dripping blob with unease. Between the brain-block balm and my current emotional state, for the first time in my death, brains didn't seem particularly appetizing.

Wind ripped through my hair as I stared at the brain. *Was this what Nerida's brain looked like now?* I thought with a shudder. I raised it up and gave it a scowl as if all of my problems were encased in this one slimy organ.

I was torn in two. Even though I couldn't smell the brain, half of me wanted to gobble it down like I usually would. My other half was repulsed at the thought of eating something that my mom and Nerida now carried around in their skulls.

Would I eat Nerida's brain if given the chance? What about my mom's? As a brain-obsessed zombie, would I even have a choice?

"So...where should we go, team?" Rick delivered the question as if we were heading out on a fun-filled family trip. From the side of my eye, I could see him and Bram nervously watching me as I stared at the brain. Then they looked at each other, exchanging the same worried glance I saw back at the Glob Theater.

I felt a wave of desperation wash through me.

"Where should we go?!" I wailed into the wind. "We have no destination! It's just the three of us, in a deathboat, drifting nowhere. Who knows what daymares may come next?"

Suddenly, as if adding a soundtrack to my angst, a death metal guitar riff blasted into the air. I nearly flinched out of my seat. When I realized the source, I exhaled in relief. It was Bram's phone.

"I can't believe I get reception out here," said Bram. He pressed the answer button and slowly brought the phone to his ear. "Hello?"

Rick and I watched as the deathboat rose and dropped along with the crashing waves. "Um, hi," said Bram. And then after a pause, "OK, sure, she's right here."

Bram handed me the phone and mouthed the words, "*It's your mom.*"

I set the brain down on the aluminum seat beside me and grimaced as it made a squelching sound. With a deep breath, I took Bram's phone. "Mom?"

"Edda…" It was my mom's smooth, non-raspy human voice. The line sputtered with static. The connection wasn't great. "…others listening in…remember who you are…committed to science and to Deadmark…"

The call was breaking up. I couldn't quite understand what

she was saying, but it felt so comforting to hear my mom's voice again. Even if it was her human voice.

"Mom, I'm so sorry," I said. "I didn't know if I could believe you at first, but now I know it's all true. Agonista is ruining our country. I should have humanized her when I had a chance."

"No, Edda," said my mom, firm but patient. "Revenge is petty…"

"That's what Nerida told me," I said quietly. A new rush of guilt pulsed through me. I glanced with disgust at the brain at my side.

"Save Deadmark," said my mom. "Unite behind science… trust friends…yourself…"

Bram's phone gave a beep of dismay. "Oh no!" said Bram. "My phone's battery is running out."

"Mom, quick—is there any-thing else I need to know?" I spoke as fast as I could. "Bram's phone won't last much longer!"

"…can't say…others listen-ing…" my mom said. Another pathetic beep from Bram's phone. "…hear this…go where…first-hand perspective."

Just as my mom spoke her last

word, Bram's phone gave three sorrowful beeps in a row and then shut off.

"I'm sorry, Edda," said Bram. "I couldn't charge it on the Ignorwegian ship. They have different outlets."

"It's fine, Bram," I said with a sigh. I handed him his depleted phone. "I just need to figure out what my mom means. Something about 'a first-hand perspective.'"

"Oooh, a riddle!" said Rick, bopping up and down in the air. "I love riddles."

The three of us rocked on the water in silence, pondering my mom's words.

It sounded like she was telling me to get a first-hand perspective, but wasn't my perspective always first hand? I suppose sometimes I received someone else's perspective second hand, but why would I have to go somewhere specific to get a first-hand perspective?

"First hand," I said, my brow wrinkled in thought. Rick floated circles around the perimeter of the boat, lost in concentration. Bram was leaning back with his head on the boat's ledge, staring into the sky.

"That's it!" I yelled, jumping up and causing the boat to rock wildly. "We need to go to the Ur-Hand statue in the Circle of Willis. It's literally a perspective of the 'first hand,' or, in other words, 'a first-hand perspective'!"

"Ah—I almost had it," said Rick, disappointed.

"But what if Agonista arrests you again?" asked Bram.

"That's a risk I'm willing to take. I didn't believe my mom before, and it made everything worse. I'm not going to make that same mistake again."

"Aye aye! That's good enough for me!" said Bram, as he revved up the deathboat's motor.

Bram steered the craft toward Deadmark, slamming into oncoming waves. As we gained momentum, Rick struggled to float next to me and keep pace with the rollercoaster ups and downs of the sea.

I stared gravely at the rushing waves and considered my mom's words. If I was correctly piecing together what she was saying, it sounded like she was again urging me to trust in science. But her own trust in science wasn't very helpful. All it gave her was a one-way ticket to Ignorway.

Nerida also trusted in science, and she was a human now, too. I knew I had to listen to my mom, and I had to do everything I could to fix this mess, but why did things have to be this way? Why were so many good zombies having their deaths ruined like this?

"Listen," said Rick, floating in closer to me. His usually jolly face was strained with concern. "I know things are hard right now, but it will get better. I mean, imagine how I felt when the Enchantress turned me into a floating skull."

A spritz of black water leaped into the boat and speckled my face. I wiped it away with my flannel sleeve.

"I was the most popular playwright and actor in Ignorway," Rick continued. "My humor was limitless. Always singing, pranking, joking. I could always get the whole theater to laugh and to cry. But when I lost my body, the humans stopped caring. It all went away."

Rick gazed toward the dark horizon. I had never really considered Rick's previous life. To me, Rick was always Rick. A floating blue skull, an excellent dramatist, a good friend.

"I thought, 'What am I now?'" he said. "My beautiful career was over. I figured I was about as useful as a bowling ball. But then, after the zombie outbreak, I moved to Deadmark to get a fresh start. The zombies accepted me as I am, I built the Glob Theater, and everything turned around for me."

"You're right, Rick. And so are Bram and my mom." I sat up a little straighter at my friend's encouragement. "Things haven't worked out well for me lately, and I haven't made all the right decisions. But I can't get sidetracked by feeling bad for myself. I need to stay strong for my mom, for Nerida, and for all of Deadmark."

Rick smiled serenely. I looked at him, and then at Bram,

who was laser-focused on the rolling waters ahead. I was happy they were my friends. And not only because they saved me from becoming werewolf food.

"Thank you both," I said, "for being the best friends a zombie could ask for, and for sticking with me through all of this madness."

"You'd do the same for us," said Bram.

"We'll always be there for you," said Rick. "You can bet your death on it."

The deathboat whizzed up and down on the waves through-out the day, into the night, and then into the next day. I did my best to focus on the sea ahead and block out the negative thoughts that stormed through my mind.

I was so wired, I couldn't sleep. Instead, I focused on Bram and Rick, two friends who stuck by me even when things got rough...*really* rough. And I focused on my mom's guiding words. If she could be optimistic as a human in a coal mine, surely I could muster up a little hope for myself.

Although I wasn't completely successful in drumming up a positive outlook, I was at least able to eat the brain Bram had so kindly nabbed from *The Quick and the Dead*. It was one of the more emotionally conflicted meals I'd ever had, but it provided some much-needed energy.

At last, the giant skull of Zømborg Castle appeared on the horizon. The menacing clock glowed through the fog as the pendulum eyes ticked away. The tick-tick-ticking of the pendulums added a layer of tension to the atmosphere, as if a bomb were ready to go off.

The thick fog blocked the wind turbines from view, and I noted with a mix of sadness and anger that I couldn't hear them either. Apparently Agonista had been busy since I left.

Bram steered the deathboat past the castle and along the rolling waves toward East Ganglia Bay. As I peered out at the coastline on the lookout for spying sentries or other signs of trouble, Rick hid low in the boat so his glowing blue light wouldn't be spotted by anyone who might be watching.

Soupy fog wrapped around us like a shroud. Luckily, this made it very difficult for anyone to see us. But it was also frightening—it meant we couldn't see very well either. Who knew what lurked in that dark haze?

Bram carefully angled the boat along the bay's northern docks. Boats and ships rocked sleepily in the fog.

There wasn't a zombie in sight as Bram gently bumped the boat alongside the dock. We'd timed our arrival so that we'd pull into port in the middle of the day, when most zombies were retired in their graves. If not for the snoring sounds drifting out from the cabin of a nearby research vessel, Deadmark would have seemed completely abandoned.

Without a sound, I hopped out and held the boat's line while Bram disembarked. I carefully tied the boat to a stone piling, steadying myself as the dock lilted up and down on the waves.

Together, the three of us crept up along the dock in silence and made our way toward Cerebrum Street. The fog was too dense to see much on either side of us, so we kept our eyes on the cobblebone road straight ahead.

Rick's blue light stained the surrounding fog. The only sounds were the padding of my bare feet and the squeaking of Bram's sneakers on the damp stone. Soon, the towering fingertips of the Ur-Hand statue emerged above the fog as we entered the Circle of Willis.

The circle felt completely deserted. Carefully, slowly, we reached the statue, and…nothing happened.

I placed my hand on the statue's base—the wrist—and wondered what we were supposed to do next. Did we get the riddle wrong? I was so sure we had it right…

I turned around to consult with Bram and Rick, and a frantic scream suddenly echoed through the fog. I covered my mouth—the scream had been mine. There was another figure standing behind Bram.

The figure stepped forward to reveal a face twisted in fury. He was so angry that I didn't recognize him at first. But then I noticed the dreadlocks and the Sourbone blazer.

It was Argo, Nerida's brother and Cabbagio's son. He looked ready to rip something apart.

With a rigid finger aimed directly at my face, he shrieked: "Humanizer!"

My head hung in shame as that awful word thundered across the circle.

CHAPTER THIRTEEN

GRINDING OF THE AX

"You humanized my entire family!" Argo shouted. He took a step toward me, and Bram moved between us.

"Relax, Argo," said Bram. "Edda didn't humanize your sister."

"Nerida never would have humanized herself if it wasn't for Edda!" Argo's finger hadn't stopped pointing at me.

"I rushed back from Sourbone after hearing what you did to my dad," said Argo. "When I got to Nerida's lab, the place was trashed, and she was missing. I found human clothes, the empty humanizer bottle, and a trail of these!"

Argo pulled cheese puffs out of his pocket and dramatically tossed them into the air.

"First you humanized my dad, which caused Nerida to humanize herself. Now you're here to humanize me." Argo paced back and forth like a detective rattling off case notes. He suddenly stopped and held up a finger as if everything had come into focus. "And you're the one who sent me that anonymous text to meet you here. It all makes perfect sense."

My feeling of dread was punctured by a loud crunch in front of me. Bram sheepishly raised his sneaker to reveal the dusty orange remnants of a crushed cheese puff. "Oops," he said.

The crunchy interruption was enough to snap me out of my stupor. I cleared my throat.

"Argo, I'm not the one who texted you," I began, cautiously. "I don't even own a phone."

I stepped around Bram to make eye contact with Argo, but he took a step back.

"I'm not going to humanize you, or anyone, ever again," I said. "Your dad's humanization was an accident, and I'm very sorry that it happened."

"That's exactly what a serial humanizer would say," Argo snapped.

"I'm not a serial humanizer, Argo." I held my hands up as if to prove I didn't have mutagen on me. "Like you, I'm heart-broken that Nerida humanized herself. In fact, you probably won't believe me, but it hurts me as much as you."

"Take it back!" cried Argo, resuming his finger pointing. "You never cared about Nerida. You have no idea the pain I'm going through! I'm so sad, I could drink gasoline, or...eat a cheese puff!"

Argo clenched his jaw and his fists. He let loose an odd moaning sound that seemed to be a demonstration of sadness. My patience had worn thin. How dare he question me? I missed Nerida just as much as he did, maybe even more!

"I've always cared about Nerida, even when we didn't get along," I said, raising my voice despite the risk of drawing someone's attention. "I would never do anything to hurt her... at least not on purpose."

Argo bent down and picked up a cheese puff. "I'll prove my sorrow by eating this," he said. "I doubt you would do the same."

I wasn't going to let Argo out-sorrow me, so I picked up a cheese puff as well. We both held our puffs near our mouths and glared at each other.

"Edda, you don't have to do this," said Bram. He put his hand on my shoulder.

Then, in a flash, Argo shoved the cheese puff into his mouth and crunched noisily. I took a deep breath and, with eyes shut tight, did the same. It was absolutely disgusting.

"It's so bad!" yelled Argo, puffy crumbs flying everywhere.

"I hate it!" I cried.

Neither of us could swallow our miserable puffs. We spat out the orange filth at the base of the Ur-Hand statue.

With watering eyes, we looked at each other. We didn't know what to do.

"OK, you two," said Rick, floating up to us. "Eating cheese puffs isn't going to do anyone any good…least of all your digestive systems. We need to be careful. We don't want to cause a scene. Or, at least, we don't want to cause an even bigger scene."

"I should challenge you to a duel," said Argo. "I've been taking fencing lessons in Franke."

"A fencing duel?" I asked with a scoff. "That's a little far-fetched." Argo responded with a scowl.

"Look, Argo," I said. "You have every right to be mad at me about your dad. It was an accident, but it was a dumb one. I shouldn't have been so careless with humanizer mutagen."

Ever so slightly, the fury of Argo's stare decreased in intensity.

"I know what it's like to lose a parent to humanization," I continued. "I would never do that on purpose."

"Edda—" Argo began. His tone sounded softer, but whatever he was about to say was abruptly interrupted by the ground rumbling beneath us.

"Look out!" cried Bram. Argo and I jumped out of the way as a trapdoor opened up in the stone where we once stood. We marveled as three more doors opened around the base of the Ur-Hand statue.

More than a dozen hooded figures crawled out of the trapdoors and surrounded us. They were expressionless ZETHs, too numerous to consider fighting.

A shorter ZETH stepped forward. Lowering their hood, the figure shook loose a crop of fluffy pink hair.

Bram yelled, Rick gasped, Argo yelped, and I groaned in shock.

It was Nerida. She was still a zombie, and her smile had never been bigger.

"Aw, you guys," she said. "Did you really eat cheese puffs for me?"

My hands shook like jackhammers the entire way down the trapdoor's ladder. My mind was sizzling with shock. It felt as though we had split from reality and entered a new dimension in which Nerida was still dead.

We lowered ourselves into what appeared to be a secret bunker carved out of the stone beneath the circle. It was filled with monitors, books, and computers.

"Welcome to the secret ZETH control room!" Nerida declared. "They built it decades ago, working in the middle of the day so no one would notice. Isn't it the coolest?"

When we hopped down from the ladder, my hands were still shaking. I reached out and touched Nerida's arm. "You're...you're dead," I stammered.

"Yes, of course," she said cheerily. "Why wouldn't I be?"

"We...we all thought you were a human," said Argo, his hands on his head. "The trashed lab...the cheese puffs...the human clothes...the missing boat."

"Right," she said tapping her chin ponderously. "The trashed lab wasn't my fault, but I could see how the rest of it looks bad."

ZETHs placed chairs beside me, Bram, and Argo. "Please," said one. "Have a seat."

Nerida sat down on a large black swivel chair in front of a bank of monitors built into the stone. She spun around to face us. I still couldn't believe she was sitting here before me in her full zombie glory. As far as I was concerned, any disagreement between us had melted away. How had I ever taken her for granted?

"First of all—Bram, Rick—I can't thank you enough for your heroism," said Nerida. "I'll never be able to repay you for whisking my dad away to safety. Please know that you have a friend for the rest of my death."

Bram's green cheeks reddened. "Ah, that? That was nothing," he said, nervously avoiding eye contact.

"It's not every day a dramatist is called a hero," said Rick with a smile. "I'll take it!"

"Now, where to begin about the lab?" said Nerida, squinting one eye in thought. "I guess it all started a few weeks ago when I attended a ZETH meeting. I had an idea that could help them with the inconveniences of cockroach eating, and I wanted to hear their perspective in general."

Nerida gestured to a ZETH protester, who came forward. Over his hood, the zombie wore a contraption that placed a bottle on each side of his head. Tubes dropped down from the bottles and into the zombie's mouth. Each bottle was adorned with the simple icon of a cockroach.

"The bottles are filled with pureed cockroaches," Nerida explained. All the ZETHs were wearing the contraptions. With all the shock from the last few minutes, I hadn't noticed

them before. "They're much more practical than shoving live cockroaches into your mouth all the time, right?"

All of the ZETHs slurped and nodded enthusiastically.

"Tangy and tolerable," said one, with a thumbs up.

"I attended one meeting, and then another," Nerida continued. "I learned more about their organization and their views on things."

"You're not a human…" Argo repeated, distantly.

"I'm so sorry to scare you like that, bro," said Nerida. "And sorry for the creepy anonymous text. We can't be too careful these days."

She walked over and put her arm around her brother. "In addition to Bram and Rick, it took many more heroic friends to make sure Dad was safe. The ZETHs stepped up immediately—without them, Dad might not be free."

Nerida made eye contact with each of us in the room, one after another. "Now, this is going to come as a shock, so bear with me." She inhaled, exhaled, and said, "The ZETHs' human rights work has led them to develop some strong allies in Ignorway—*human* allies."

Human *allies*? My mind wavered. I couldn't believe what I was hearing. Those two words just don't belong together. It was an oxymoron, an inherent contradiction. Like "sweet sorrow" or "vegan werewolf."

"Wild, right?" said Nerida, nodding in agreement with our shock.

"So a few ZETHs volunteered to take my boat to Ignorway to rescue Dad," she continued. "The cheese puffs and human clothes were for Dad, not me. I wanted to make sure he was comfortable and fed, no matter what condition the ZETHs found him in. The PlayThings helped me collect some human clothes from the Glob Theater, and I made the artificial cheese puffs in the lab. It's the only human food I could make with the chemicals I had in stock."

Nerida gestured to the monitors on the wall. "Then the ZETHs motored off to Ignorway and I stayed in touch from the ZETH control room."

"And the bottle of humanizer?" asked Rick.

"I poured the last remaining bottle into the hazardous materials container in my lab and added some destructive chemicals to render the mutagen inert," said Nerida. "I wanted to ensure no one would be humanized again—either on purpose or on accident. I just didn't have time to recycle the bottle."

Nerida shook her head. "And good thing I got rid of it. Someone trashed my lab when I was out—Agonista must have been looking for more mutagen after she saw Dad get humanized."

"So dad's really a human?" Argo asked. "I can't believe it...

it's just so *gross*."

"Yes, Argo," said Nerida. "But at least he exists. The ZETHs were able to rescue him from a coal mine near the city of Causewoe. Their human allies helped them find it. Apparently, it's where all unregistered humans are sent."

"Waaait…the coal mine in Causewoe?" I asked, suddenly dizzy. This was way too much shocking information to handle at once. But even with the flood of surprise, I began to connect a few dots.

I took a wobbly step toward my former lab partner. "Nerida, how did my mom know to direct me to the Ur-Hand statue?"

Nerida walked to the bank of monitors, clicked a button, and said, "Why don't you ask her yourself?"

CHAPTER FOURTEEN

COMPELLED VALOR

The monitor flickered awake, and there she was. My human mom and those bright green eyes.

She wore the same dirty denim jumpsuit, but she had ditched the hardhat and washed the coal smudges off her face.

Beside her stood the shiny-headed human form of Cabbagio. He was wearing a green tracksuit. His so-called Power Gems were nowhere to be seen.

"Mom!" I cried.

"Dad!" cried Argo.

Nerida stepped away as we both moved toward the screens.

"I'm sorry I couldn't tell you everything on the phone, Edda," my mom said. "It was too risky to communicate directly.

Agonista is becoming more and more paranoid, and I was worried she or the Shadow Council might be listening in. Thankfully, this ZETH video feed is fully encrypted, so nobody can intercept our call."

The room was spinning. I placed a hand on the control panel to steady myself. *My mom is in cahoots with Nerida and the ZETHs…and Cabbagio? Something about a Shadow Council?* Nerida slid a chair behind me, lowered me down, and patted my shoulder.

Argo, too, was reeling from new information. "Wait, the former Lead Scientist is a human? And the current Lead Scientist is bad? I had no idea…" Nerida patiently brought Argo up to speed as he shook his head in disbelief. "She was so convincing," he said.

"Yes, my sister is a very talented liar," said my mom. "But, thankfully, we have truth on our side—and on both sides of the Undead Sea."

What my mom said next only heightened our collective astonishment.

"Through their human rights work," she continued, "the ZETHs connected with a group of brave young humans who are just as concerned about the future of Ignorway as we are about the future of Deadmark. They're scientists, like us."

The concept of human allies was hard enough to handle

on its own. But human *scientists*? My mind wasn't ready for this rupture in my understanding of the world.

The lens on their video feed began moving to the right. Like I was watching a horror movie, I covered my face and peered through my fingers.

The camera revealed a group of human children—about my age—sitting around a table that was covered in science equipment and stacks of paper.

I gasped.

Bram said, "Whaaat?"

Argo seemed to gag a little.

The humans all wore lab coats, and some had goggles resting on top of their heads. Their lab outfits were similar to what a zombie scientist might wear. Each of the humans met our gaze with calm curiosity.

Along with an array of gas masks, a group of ZETHs lined the wall behind them. They slurped away on their cockroach puree helmet tubes.

One of the children offered a self-conscious wave before the camera returned to my mom and Cabbagio.

"After Bram and Rick saved me from the zombies of Deadmark, these brave kids and the ZETHs rescued us from that awful coal mine," said Cabbagio. "I can't thank you all enough. It's much more kindness than I deserve. I owe you all my death—" Cabbagio grimaced, realizing his error. "Oops, I mean *life*."

A ZETH stepped up next to me. "Every human deserves kindness," she said. "Our commitment to human rights means we're not only dedicated to saving humans from zombies—but also to saving humans from themselves. That's why we have to figure out a way to end the Ignorwegian obsession with fossil fuels. It's unhealthy and destructive. For all of us."

"And we want the same thing," said one of the human scientists, walking into view.

She adjusted her goggles and hugged a clipboard close to her chest. "We could easily hate zombies for constantly attacking Ignorway and eating our brains, but the problem posed by climate change is much larger than zombie attacks. I mean, we can't even go outside anymore without wearing these." She held up a gas mask with a look of disgust. "Our generation of humans deserves better."

"The same goes for zombies," said Nerida. "It's time we all worked together to end the devastation. We share the same world, after all."

I cradled my reeling head in my hands, and Nerida again patted my shoulder consolingly. It felt as if my entire death had been a lie up to this point. These humans were clearly not the goonish buffoons I had carried in my mind's eye.

They seemed committed, intelligent, and morally strong. If I was being honest, they almost reminded me of myself…before things got out whack.

"Excuse me," said Bram. "This has been quite the rollercoaster of information. I do have one quick question…I may have misheard you, but did you say something about a Shadow Council?"

My mom looked at Cabbagio, who seemed to tear up. He gulped down his sorrow and cleared his throat.

"Agonista has a group of human executives from Choke Industries installed in the Lead Scientist's quarters," he said. "In Edda's old graveroom, actually. That's who she's always talking to through her earpiece, and they're the ones who have been helping her spread lies about science and climate change across Deadmark."

The shocks just kept coming. I was very glad to be sitting down. My imagination tormented me with visions of creepy human executives lurking in my closet.

"I was so misguided and wrong," said Cabbagio, voice trembling.

Almost as astonishing as the news itself was that it came from Agonista's former Chief of Staff. I looked into Cabbagio's unnerving but sincere human eyes, and a wave of guilt washed over me.

"I'm so sorry for humanizing you," I said. "It was a complete accident, but I was careless—"

"No, Edda," said Cabbagio, bowing his head slightly. "It is I who should apologize to you. I was led astray by Agonista's lies. Your mom has set me straight. Spending time with her has helped me remember what a real leader looks like."

Argo put his hand on my shoulder. Even among the recent shockwaves, their forgiveness meant everything to me. It felt like a weight the size of Zømborg Castle had been airlifted off of my head.

"Cabbagio has recommitted himself to the scientific ideals on which Deadmark was founded," said my mom with poise worthy of a Lead Scientist.

Softly to himself, Cabbagio whispered, "The Power Gems did nothing…"

"It's these ideals that will get us out of this mess," said my mom. "Nothing else can."

"Exactly," said Nerida, clapping her hands to punctuate her enthusiasm. "The humans will work on their end, and we'll work here in the ZETH control room. We can collaborate through this encrypted video feed. Together, the brightest zombies and humans can find a solution." Nerida smiled broadly. "And we'll find it with science."

"Your words are a rhapsody to my earholes!" cried Rick with a joyful twirl.

"I'm not sure what 'rhapsody' means, but I'm in," said Bram.

My friends looked at me for a response, but all I could muster was a slow and silent nod. I agreed with my mom and Nerida, theoretically, but it was going to take some adjusting to get used to this new acceptance of humans.

"Oh, but there's one thing first," said my mom. "You should probably rescue the Elected Council. I know them well—they were easily deceived and weak-willed, but they're not bad zombies."

"Oh, right, them," said Nerida, rolling her eyes.

"With all we have going on, are they really worth the effort?" asked a ZETH behind me. "Even if they're not evil, they still failed Deadmark. And all it took was an all-you-can-eat buffet of swanky brains and bubbly brain fluid."

"I also failed Deadmark," said Cabbagio. "I may never gain your trust, but I'll spend the rest of my human life trying."

"What Cabbagio and the Elected Council did is almost unforgiveable," said my mom. "And they should be held to account with a ReConstitutional trial. But for now, saving them from potential harm is the right thing to do. We have to be true to our values, no matter what."

It felt wrong to show compassion to the gluttonous, self-centered Elected Council. But deep down, in my heart of hearts, I knew my mom was right. Compassion, not vengeance, was the way out of this mess.

"I know they're in secret dungeons beneath the castle," I said. "But I have no idea how to get there."

A ZETH protester raised her hand. "We know the way to the secret dungeons," she said, matter-of-factly.

"OK, fine," said Nerida with a shrug. "I guess we should rescue those upstanding public servants."

"Yeah," I said. "I suppose we can squeeze it in."

We made our way through a stone cavern that connected the ZETH control room to a series of tunnels beneath the castle.

Bram, Nerida, Argo, and I wore black ZETH hoodies with our hoods up. We blended in nicely with the group of ZETHs who accompanied us. Rick hovered in front, his blue light illuminating our path.

"I have to admit, Nerida," I said. "You've really done a great job of bringing everyone together."

"Yeah, I know," she said with a smirk. "I mean, someone

needed to take action. Not all of us have time to skip around singing weird pop songs."

I winced, but Nerida was right. She was always ready to tell me exactly how things were. Which is what best friends do.

The ZETH in front held up a hand in the middle of the cavern. We all stopped. He reached for a nondescript skull at waist level in the middle of the wall. The ZETH used two fingers to poke the skull's eyes sockets and placed a thumb in the skull's mouth. Then he turned it like a doorknob.

Rick grunted with sympathy as the ZETH pushed the skull forward. It was attached to a camouflaged door made of plaster that was painted to look like the surrounding stone.

"The secret dungeons are down this tunnel to the left," said the ZETH as we all followed him into an even darker, danker cavern than the one before.

As we approached the turn, a ZETH cut us off. She held a hand out in front of us and put a finger to her mouth to silently communicate "stop and listen."

There were footsteps coming toward us on the other side of the bend. Before I had time to process our options, Rick zipped around the corner with a wild scream. "*Ayiyiyiyiyiyi!*"

A commotion of yells, grunts, and moans erupted around the corner. After a moment of startled hesitation, we all scrambled around the turn to see what had happened.

Rick's blue light illuminated two figures: Squeak and Gibber. Squeak had fallen out of his harness and stood on the ground, raising both arms in surrender. Gibber was lying on his side, holding his stomach in pain.

Behind them stood the seven members of the Elected Council. Their traditional robes were caked in grime, and their cheeks were hollowed with hunger.

"Don't hurt us!" yelled Squeak. Gibber groaned in pain.

"And why shouldn't we?" said Rick, clearly revved up with adrenaline. "You deserve so much more than a flying skull in the stomach."

"Because we ain't the villains anymore," said Squeak. ZETHs approached the brain-hunting zombies and took their weapons away. Neither resisted.

Still on the ground, Gibber blared something that nobody could understand, except Squeak.

Squeak nodded. "Yes, Gibber's right. After the humans took *The Quick and the Dead*, we began rowing our way back to Deadmark. Agonista had given us a sealed envelope to deliver to the werewolves. Even though we lost Edda and our ship, I opened the envelope to see if there was some way we could save our mission, if even just a little bit."

He pulled an envelope from his pocket. "Here," said Squeak, handing it to me. "Read it for yourself."

I removed a notecard with a message written in prickly letters. Rick floated over my shoulder, and I read it aloud:

DEAR WEREWOLVES,
PLEASE EAT EVERYONE ON BOARD THIS SHIP.
EVEN THE TALL ONE AND THE SHORT ONE
ON THE TALL ONE'S SHOULDERS. FEEL FREE
TO KEEP THE SHIP OR BURN IT DOWN FOR
ALL I CARE.
GOOD DOGS,
—AGONISTA, LEAD SCIENTIST OF DEADMARK

Gibber blared again at my reading of the letter. Squeak bowed his head in shame.

"This note made Gibber and me reconsider everything," said Squeak. "Agonista made us feel important, but she never actually cared about us at all. She was a strong business-zombie, and she promised to make us rich and influential just like her. But it turned out she only cared about her own power and wealth. We were more than deceived."

Gibber mumbled in regretful tones, and Squeak said, "Yes, Gibber. We now know Edda was right about democracy. It's the way to go."

"Brains?" asked one of the council members. "So hungry…"

"How about some cockroach puree?" said a ZETH, handing his helmet to the council member. "You get used to the taste... eventually."

"Cockroaches?" muttered a council member, staring at the helmet in stunned disappointment.

Squeak cleared his throat. "As we rowed back to Deadmark, Gib and I discussed ways to make things right. We realized that freeing the Elected Council was a pretty good start. They were thrown into the dungeon when they began to question Agonista. We knew they were misled and tricked, just like us."

Gibber mumbled again. Squeak said, "Yes, we're very sorry. We're sorry for spying on you to find the mutagen's hiding place, Nerida. And we're sorry for stealing a bottle. And Edda, we're sorry that we chased your mom after Agonista humanized her, and for trying to deliver you to the werewolves."

Squeak paused in thought. "Now that I say it out loud, we really did a lot of bad things. Mostly, I guess we're just sorry for trusting Agonista and letting her influence us like that."

I looked at Nerida, Bram, and Argo. They all shrugged back at me in unison. "Well," I said, "welcome to the resistance, I guess. But you're going to have to earn our trust. You can start by telling us everything you know about Agonista's plans."

Gibber slowly got to his feet and moaned sentences of unknown meaning. Squeak listened patiently and nodded.

"Yup, we know we have a lot of making up to do," he said. "And we're ready to do whatever it takes. Unfortunately, we don't know much about Agonista's plan, except she's been holed up in her quarters trying to figure out the formula for humanizer mutagen. Whatever she's planning, it definitely involves more humanizations."

My mental gears were cranking. "So Agonista doesn't know you know that she tried to have you devoured?"

"Nope," said Squeak. "After rowing here, we came straight to the secret dungeons."

"Hmm," I said, tapping the side of my cheek. "Let's get back to the ZETH control room. I have a plan brewing. I think there's a way we can play my aunt like a pipe."

I pulled out the lab notes Nerida had given me in her undersea garden. I held them up in the air like a beacon. "The answer has been with us all along—and the answer is science."

Looking at Nerida, I tried my best to steady my voice. "Our oath was right the whole time. Science *is* the key to future zombie peace. And I'll never doubt it again."

"Now that's what I'm talking about!" cried Nerida. "The princess is taking action!"

"Hey, Nerida?" I said.

"Yes?" she replied with fake innocence.

"Don't call me 'princess'."

For the next forty-eight hours, we barely ate and hardly slept. In collaboration with the humans in Ignorway, we nurtured and expanded upon my spark of a plan.

And, incredibly, the humans were admirable partners. Every now and then I was struck with a twinge of heebie-jeebies when I looked at them through the video screen and saw their plump cheeks and shiny hair. But their plucky professionalism won me over.

My former self would have been flabbergasted to learn that Edda, devourer of brains and despiser of humans, would one day form an alliance of science with her primary food source. The world never ceases to bewilder.

At first I was shocked, but then it became oddly natural. It wasn't that the world had changed, even though it felt like it—it was my perception that had changed. My understanding became more evolved, more nuanced.

I had always thought of humans as mindless weirdos, but I had just been taking the easy way out. Had I thought of humans as committed firefighters or doctors or artists—let alone scientists—it would have made every meal a lot more conflicted. Blocking out those complexities made my death easier, but it did not reflect reality.

So, as respected equals, everyone played a crucial role in our plan, whether zombie, human, vampire, or floating skull. Before, we only knew our individual strength. It wasn't until our plan took shape that we began to understand what we could become together.

For two nights, we honed our strategy, fine-tuned our tactics, assigned roles and responsibilities, and never looked back. Nothing was going to get in our way.

Even though so much was riding on our work, I was able to disappear into the task at hand. Despite the looming threat of Agonista and her Shadow Council, the bad feelings temporarily dissolved in a flurry of beakers, lab notes, computer screens, and whiteboard drawings.

But most of all, it felt wonderful to be working elbow-to-elbow with Nerida once again. Our minds fused together like they used to. As if we had never skipped a beat.

No matter how it turned out, for those hours in the ZETH control room, all was right with the world.

CHAPTER FIFTEEN

TREASON! TREASON!

"**S**tep right up, folks! Come feast your eyes on the show of the millennium!"

Three nights later, Rick zoomed around the Circle of Willis wearing a wireless headset microphone. His voice roared through speakers as he zipped around with passionate zest. Pumping up a crowd was truly his superpower.

I stood on stage with Bram, Nerida, and Argo. While Deadmark slept through the day, we worked hard to construct a temporary stage in front of the Ur-Hand statue. We couldn't have done it without the stagecraft mastery of Rick and the Play Things leading the way.

Large spotlights swooped back and forth, sending towering

columns of light into the darkness above. For the first night in weeks, there wasn't a pollution flake or acid raindrop in the sky.

We had strung colorful bunting flags across rooftops and through the fingers of the Ur-Hand statue. Around the circle, on balconies and on light posts, we had hoisted large monitors and speakers so everyone could witness the show.

The biggest monitor was above us, fastened into the Ur-Hand's palm. All of the screens flashed images of delicious brains with the text *"FREE BRAINS! FREE BRAINS!"* It was quite the spectacle.

The Play Things were spread out across the Circle of Willis and beyond, drumming up interest and handing out flyers that further advertised *"FREE BRAINS!"* Together, they funneled the crowd into the large viewing area we had roped off in front of the Ur-Hand statue.

It felt a little shameless to lure zombies in with the promise of free brains—an offer no zombie could resist. But we were willing to take anyone who would give us their attention. The more zombie eyeballs, the better. We were going to expose Agonista in front of everyone—and this time, Agonista would portray herself.

Even though Agonista's lies and misinformation had created false disagreements among zombies, the need for brains was a great unifier. When it came to brains, it didn't matter where a particular zombie stood on a particular issue. We all just wanted to gorge.

As the crowd formed before us, Squeak and Gibber appeared on the cobblebone path by the circle's northeast entrance. Gibber clutched one of the flyers. Subtly, barely perceptibly, they both nodded to me in unison.

I nodded back as they walked away to deliver the flyer to our target. I looked up above them. Two Play Things were stationed on a building's rooftop overlooking the circle.

Among the roof's various turbines and barometers, they had assembled an assortment of audio-visual equipment. One of them wore a Krampus mask, and the other wore an elf mask. The Krampus mask flashed a red light in our direction.

That was the signal. It was time to begin.

"Yo, Rick!" I yelled. "Let's start the show!"

Rick floated down and gently bumped foreheads with Bram, Nerida, Argo, and then me. "Let's break a leg...uh, you know what I mean."

With a laugh, he shot up and zoomed high above the crowd. His voice bellowed through the speakers. "Zombies! I must request your attention, please! In fact—I demand it!"

The hungry groans from the crowd turned into light muttering as everyone zeroed their attention in on Rick. "These days, I know it seems that an honest zombie is but one in ten thousand. It feels impossible to have faith in one another—but we must. It's easy to deceive, and much harder to trust. But that's exactly what I'm asking you to do right now—join me in trusting this young zombie with your deaths. I promise you, she speaks nothing but the truth."

Up on the rooftop, the elf-masked Play Thing aimed his camera at me. Behind us on stage, a Play Thing wearing a triceratops mask sat at a small table with a laptop. A few keystrokes later and suddenly my face was plastered across all the monitors in the circle.

Whispers and chatter traveled across the crowd. This is the first time they had seen me since I was allegedly banished by the Elected Council.

I flicked on the megaphone and looked at Nerida. She nodded back with firm encouragement.

The megaphone screeched and squawked with feedback as I brought it to my mouth. I heard some laughter skitter through the crowd. I ignored it. Nothing was going to interfere with what I had to say.

"Zombies of Deadmark!" I said, strong and clear. "I was not banished by the Elected Council, as many of you were led to believe. That is just one example in a long list of lies we have been fed. Fellow zombies, I am here to tell you that we've been hoodwinked! We've been steered away from Deadmark's

founding principles!"

There was some clapping and a few boos. But everyone was paying attention. "We have been guided away from science," I continued, "and down a path of destruction."

I heard a few key taps behind me, and the monitors switched feeds. They now showed the Elected Council, who were being filmed beneath us in the ZETH control room.

The Elected Council had traded their grimy robes for normal zombie clothing like ripped shirts and raggedy jeans and skirts. They looked a little healthier than they did when we met them in the caverns, but they were still a far cry from their formerly pampered selves.

The crowd chattered in confusion—it was quite shocking to see the Elected Council dressed in street clothes.

"Agonista deceived the Elected Council, distracting them with expensive brain delicacies and bubbly brain fluid," I declared. "When they questioned her motives, she threw them into the dungeon. She took them out of the decision-making process, and your democracy was taken with it."

I surveyed the bloodshot eyeballs peering at me from the crowd. In some I could see confusion, in others sympathy. In many, I saw only a hunger for brains.

"Edda is speaking the truth," said a council member on the screen, head bowed in shame. "We're so very sorry."

"Agonista deceived us and lured us away from our obligations to Deadmark," said another with tears in his eyes. "We didn't know she was behind the anti-science movement, and we didn't know she was destroying our country's renewable technology." His voice cracked with emotion. "But we should have been smarter. We should have been stronger. Deadmark deserves so much better."

Then, from the circle's northeast entrance, Agonista walked forward with Squeak and Gibber at her side.

The Krampus-masked Play Thing gave me a thumbs up and then illuminated Agonista with the spotlight's blazing eye. The elf-masked Play Thing aimed a long-range microphone at Agonista to make sure that if she had anything to say, all of Deadmark would hear it.

Agonista had a duffel bag around her shoulder. Squeak and Gibber had machetes out, fierce and threatening as ever.

"Treason! Treason!" Argo attempted to get a chant going, but the zombie crowd wasn't ready.

"OK, Edda," said Nerida with a hint of nerves. "Now get to the punchline."

"Zombies of Deadmark!" I roared into the megaphone. "I present to you your rightful Lead Scientist, back from the beyond."

The triceratops Play Thing pressed a laptop key. The

monitors switched off the Elected Council and onto my mom's human face.

As if with one voice, the entire crowd cried out in horror. Some gagged, others turned away. Seeing their Lead Scientist as a human was the last thing they expected. I knew exactly how they felt.

"This can't be!" screamed Agonista from across the circle. "You fools said you ate her brain!"

She turned to berate Squeak and Gibber, but they were no longer at her side. "Where did you go?" she screamed, whipping her head around to find them. But they had disappeared into the crowd.

Glaring up at my mom on the screen, Agonista was all alone beneath the spotlight. Just like we wanted her.

Until that moment, I worried that Squeak and Gibber would either betray us or find a way to bungle up their part of the plan. But now, with Agonista exposed and vulnerable, I could breathe a sigh of relief: they did everything we asked of them.

Another keystroke from behind me, and the monitors were divided into split screens—one half showed Agonista, and the other half remained on my mom.

"Dear zombies of Deadmark," my mom began. "A few months ago, I was humanized by my sister—and your current

Lead Scientist—Agonista. But what she did to me is nothing compared to what she has done to our beloved country."

My mom's voice echoed throughout the circle. "She has stoked the fires of anti-science ignorance and greed. She has betrayed our entire country...for money."

"Blah blah blah!" heckled Agonista. "No one buys your lovey-dovey science nonsense. That ship has sailed!"

"I ask you, zombies of Deadmark, to unite behind science," my mom continued. "Come together and save your climate, save your country, save the world!"

The sound of solitary clapping echoed out from the circle. It was Agonista, clapping sarcastically.

"Cute plan, sister!" she snarled with spittle flying out of her mouth. The spotlight and camera followed her as she walked to the middle of the crowd. Zombies cleared out of the way out of fear, or respect, or maybe both. "You think you're so smart, but I bet you can't guess what I'm about to do next."

With the smile of a possessed clown, Agonista raised a hand to her head. She turned to stare directly into the camera. Slowly, devilishly, she removed her sunglasses.

My horror-struck scream blended with everyone else's. The camera shook a little as the elf Play Thing struggled to keep it together.

The screens were now filled with two sets of sparkling green human eyes—my mom's and my aunt's.

Agonista soaked in our reactions, cackling with evil delight. "What, you thought the sunglasses were a fashion statement? Fools!"

Nerida and I exchanged a look of panic. This was not at all part of the plan. As I struggled to gulp down my dread, Agonista peeled off a flaky latex mask to reveal a human nose beneath.

She began terrorizing the crowd with exaggerated blinks and winks into the camera. The zombie shrieks and cries worsened as she used her bony fingers to stretch her eyelids open and pull at her nose.

"Oh, get over it," she said as she removed her wireless earpiece and pulled off her hair. She dropped her wig to the ground and used her hands to puff out lush, curly, jet-black human hair.

"I humanized myself right after I humanized you, sister— with the same batch, in fact," she screamed. Her voice was smoothed out like my mom's and missing its usual metallic crackle. "As the leader of Choke Industries, it was getting way too impractical to apply brain-block balm before every board meeting. Plus, zombies can be so disgustingly idealistic."

She kicked at her white-haired wig. "Idealistic, but not very bright," she said. "Not only was I able to deceive your minds with anti-science lies, I was able to deceive your eyes, noses, and ears. All it took was some sunglasses, some cartoonish makeup, a wig lined with scent-blocking lead, and an earpiece to disguise my voice."

She paused with consideration. "OK, that's a lot of stuff, but still—you were all fooled!"

"Braaaains?...Free braaaains?" With the lead wig removed, the zombies in the crowd began to smell Agonista's human brain. She didn't have much longer before she'd become somebody's lunch.

"Back off, you filthy corpses!" she yelled. "Or I'll humanize the lot of you!"

The zombies began to close in on her, but they all stopped when she pulled a glass globe out of her duffel bag. It was filled with sparkly pink goo.

"Actually," she yelled. "I'm going to humanize you either way. That's why I made this humanization bomb." Panicked zombies moaned with fear as they stumbled into each other in an attempt to get away.

Agonista began pressing buttons on the side of the glass globe. She was activating the bomb, just as she threatened.

And for once, my aunt wasn't lying.

CHAPTER SIXTEEN

THIS IS I, EDDA THE DEAD

"**A**gonista, you don't have to be the bad guy!" It was my mom. The screens remained split between the two sisters.

Agonista held the bomb up above her head, ready to throw it into the crowd of fleeing zombies.

"Ha!" she yelled. "That's easy for you to say. You were always so moralistic. The perfect goody-goody zombie. I was never like you. I was born a villain!"

A few of the braver, hungrier zombies staggered toward Agonista, but she waved the humanizer bomb at them to keep them back.

"But at least now I'll be the most obscenely rich villain of all time," she yelled. "As Lead Scientist, I have already signed away the rights to the vast reserves of oil beneath Deadmark to Choke Industries. And as the leader of Choke Industries, I stand to make trillions."

"Agonista, please," said my mom. "You don't have to sell out your entire country for money."

"I don't have to, but I reeeally want to," growled Agonista. "Once all the zombies become humans, the ReConstitution will no longer matter. That silly document begins with the words, 'We the *zombies* of Deadmark.' If there are no zombies, there is no ReConstitution. And then the oil is mine!"

Nerida grabbed the megaphone. "No!" she yelled. "The ReConstitution will always matter. The ReConstitution also states that science is the answer—through science, and through collaboration, we can find a way forward."

"I agree, you strange little sea urchin. Science *is* the answer!" cried Agonista. "But not the answer you're hoping for. You were foolish enough to let Squeak and Gibber steal your science notebooks. For once, those dunces didn't mess it up. The notebooks were a treasure trove of helpful ideas."

She was overcome by laughter and had to compose herself before she could continue. "It was just too perfect," she gloated. "I followed your designs to make this bomb, and I followed your formula for the lovely humanizer mutagen inside it. And now that I have the recipe, I can make all the mutagen I need to make sure there are no zombies left!"

Possessed by another fit of laughter, Agonista needed several deep breaths before she could resume her monologue.

"I mean, *really?*" she screeched. "You actually had the bomb designs and the humanizer formula on back-to-back pages just waiting for me to put two and two together. How could you be so careless? You designed your bomb to spread fertilizer across the seafloor, but I have something else in mind. Something a little more *impactful.*"

"This is your last chance to reconsider, Agonista," pleaded my mom. "Mass humanization doesn't have to be in your future."

"No way, sis," said Agonista. "My business sense is too strong to pass up a flawless opportunity like this."

The glass orb in Agonista's hands gave three small beeps, causing a swell of panic among the escaping zombies. They were packed in so tight that they weren't able to make much progress in their frantic attempts to get away.

"Ah, well. It's been great catching up, but I have to throw this bomb now," said Agonista. "I want to see the humanizations up close. Trust me, sister—watching you transform was the most fun I've had in years."

She looked at the bomb's control panel and cackled fiendishly as she pushed some more buttons.

When the bomb gave a sad-sounding beep, her devilish grin transformed into a confused frown.

"What was that?" she asked no one in particular.

As she stared down at the bomb, a dinky puff of green gas shot upward, right into her face. She dropped the bomb in a fit of sputtering coughs.

"What is happening!?" screeched Agonista as she rolled on the ground, grunting in discomfort. "Am I hurt? Am I dead?" All the screens switched to focus solely on her. The zombies stopped trying to flee and gawked up at her writhing form.

Instead of the bright sparkles that had glittered across Cabbagio, Agonista's body was covered in green wisps of steam.

Nerida and I exchanged a glance. "Maybe not the answer you were looking for, Agonista?" yelled Nerida. "A real scientist would have recognized that fake information from miles away."

With curling green steam wrapping around her body, Agonista began to tremble. The quaking grew more and more intense until, suddenly, *POOF!* All at once, like a popbrain kernel bursting on a skillet, Agonista was transformed into a tiny skittering cockroach.

On stage, we jumped and high-fived and pumped our fists in celebration. Nerida, Bram, Argo, and I hugged and laughed with relief. Thankfully, our cockroachifier mutagen worked, despite Agonista's secret humanity. It was yet another instance of the same lesson I kept learning over the past few days: As it turns out, humans and zombies weren't so different after all.

We all looked up at the sound of helicopter blades in the distance. "Agonista's getaway chopper, right on time," said Bram. He gave us a peace sign, poofed into a bat, and flapped away toward a black helicopter that had crested over the castle wall on its way toward us. Rick zipped up to fly at Bram's side.

I smiled at the skull and bat rushing toward the helicopter. Thanks to intel from Squeak and Gibber, we knew it was the Shadow Council on their way to rescue Agonista. Those humans were in for a series of surprises, and Bram and Rick were the perfect welcoming committee.

Down below, Gibber walked up on one side of the cockroach, ready with a jar. Squeak walked up from the other side and, with arms stretched out, corralled the insect toward his friend. Gibber bent down and easily scooped her up.

"Sorry, Auntie," I said into the megaphone. "We must be cruel to be kind. Some time spent as a cockroach should really help put things into perspective for you. And, anyway, it's like you said—We'll all end up in the same place anyway. Zombies, humans, even cockroaches."

Squeak hopped back into his harness on Gibber's shoulders and the two made their way to the stage. Confused and anxious zombie faces watched the feared brain hunters carry their cockroach Lead Scientist through the crowd.

Zombie groans and murmurs gained volume as they puzzled through what had just happened.

Argo was on my left and Nerida on my right. Both were grinning victoriously. I put my arms around their shoulders, kicked myself into the air, and whooped with glee. Agonista was a harmless cockroach. We were out of her evil clutches, and I couldn't help but feel a rush of freedom.

"It's not time to celebrate quite yet," said Nerida. "Time for phase two. You ready?"

"You know it," I said, as I held up the megaphone.

Nerida pulled a large conch shell out of her satchel. Holding it with both hands, she blared a deafening note across the crowd. Instantly, the zombie chatter stopped.

"The era of zombies versus humans is over," I said into the megaphone, screens throughout the circle broadcasting my image. "If we're going to conquer climate change and save our shared world, we must work together. I ask that you trust in me, as I trust in you."

We had the crowd's attention. They seemed to have moved beyond shock and into a motionless kind of stupor.

"I stand before you today with only our future in mind," I said, as ZETHs climbed up on stage to stand behind me. "I have no ulterior motives, no secret tricks. This is not an imposter. This is not another faker or scam artist. This is I, Edda the Dead, demanding that we adapt. Demanding that we progress together. Demanding that we embrace humans—not as our food, but as our partners."

The ZETHs cheered loudly. There was a smattering of boos from the crowd, but mostly silence.

Nerida took the megaphone. "We promised you free brains, and, unlike a certain former Lead Scientist of ours, we would never lie to you." She looked at me, and I nodded back. "OK team," she yelled. "Roll 'em out!"

From all directions, lines of wheelbarrow-pushing Play Things and ZETHs marched into the circle. Within each wheelbarrow was a pile of jiggly, squishy, squelching brains.

They made their way to the middle of the crowd where a green stain marked the ground where Agonista once stood.

The zombies looked at the brains and looked at each other. They seemed to be wondering if this was too good to be true, if it was all a way-too-obvious trap.

"Braaains? Freee braaains?" Curious groans spread through

the crowd. The sight and smell were getting to them, but they were frozen with doubt.

"My fellow zombies," said Nerida, "we present to you FeignBrain. It's a lab-grown brain developed by zombies and humans together. We have combined human stem cells with aquatic plants, algae, and brain coral to create this wonderful new food. And no humans were harmed in its making!"

The zombies were hesitant, as we expected. From the stage, like a magician before a trick, Argo demonstratively held up a large FeignBrain for the whole crowd to see. Then he took an enormous, juicy bite.

I took a big bite of one as well. "Isn't this delicious, team?" I said into the megaphone as soggy specks sailed from my mouth.

Nerida grabbed the megaphone with FeignBrain fluid dripping down her chin. "Mmmm, it sure is, Edda! This is truly one of the best-tasting brains I've ever had. It's just like cracking open a fresh skull for the first time!"

"Braaainsss!? Freeee braaaiins!" The crowd was still hesitant, but a few of the more adventurous zombies moved closer to the wheelbarrows. The camera shifted to them.

"Dive in!" said Nerida as the zombies closed in. "Trust your eyes and your nose—they aren't deceiving you."

A brainmonger walked up and carefully surveyed a FeignBrain using a jeweler's eyeglass. She gave it a sniff, and

then a lick. Nodding to herself, she took a nibble, then a full bite. A grin broke across her face and she devoured it whole.

The crowd erupted in ravenous cheers. The Play Things and ZETHs excitedly handed out brains to the zombies in the crowd while Nerida, Argo, and I tossed them down from the stage.

"OK, please don't get frenzied," I said into the megaphone. "Nice and orderly, there are plenty of brains for everyone."

Nerida put her arm around me, and I put my head on her shoulder. Together, we watched as the zombies wolfed down dozens of FeignBrains before our eyes.

Despite a few hiccups along the way, our plan had worked. Our lab notes had been the key all along. The knowledge we acquired while making a brain-eating plant had given us a huge head start in developing a lab-grown brain.

Nerida, Bram, Argo, and I had led the science work from Deadmark, while my mom and the humans contributed heroically from Ignorway. And, although Rick wasn't the most scientifically gifted skull around, he had already come up with a snappy slogan for FeignBrain: "Make your next meal a no-brainer!"

Watching the crowd gobble brain after brain, I knew I should have never lost faith in science. And I should have never lost faith in my friends.

Just then, Bram rejoined us on stage, cheeks flushed with excitement. "I hypnotized the Shadow Council!" he cried. "Mrs. Caligari is going to be so impressed. It was just like we planned: I hypnotized the pilot from outside the helicopter, I made him land, and then I hypnotized the rest of them." Bram paused in consideration. "Actually, let's not tell Mrs. Caligari that I did any of that. She might tell my mom."

Behind Bram slouched a very dazed-looking group of seven humans, expressionless and calm. The humans wore business attire, large black sunglasses, and wireless earpieces similar to Agonista's.

"You are getting so good at that!" said Rick, clearly impressed by his friend. "I knew you'd get the hang of it."

One of the business-humans seemed to snap out of his spell. He began babbling. "We're so sorry, please don't eat our brains...we'll write a check, or give you shares of Choke—anything, please!"

"Sorry, bud," I said. "You can't bribe your way out of this one."

"Don't worry," said one of the ZETHs. "We'll be sure to put you in the coziest dungeon Deadmark has to offer. You'll have all the cockroach puree you can eat—We have loads of it we don't need anymore." The ZETHs laughed as they marched the Shadow Council away to the dungeon.

"Oh, and one more thing, Edda," said Bram with a smile. "You have a phone call."

He handed me his phone, and Bram, Nerida, Rick, Argo, and I huddled together to see my mom's beaming human face.

"Wonderful work, team," she said. "I'm so proud of each and every one of you. Now more than ever, I'm certain that Deadmark's future is in competent, compassionate hands— your hands."

"I assume that's a metaphor," quipped Rick with pretend outrage.

My mom laughed and continued. "The ReConstitution clearly states that the Lead Scientist position is for a zombie. Since I'm a human, and Agonista is a cockroach awaiting trial, it seems that a special election is the only answer. My vote no longer counts, but it's my opinion that we need some fresh blood around here to guide us into a new era. We need younger, more nimble leadership that's ready for today's challenges."

"I think she's talking about us," said Nerida. We both laughed.

"But we'll figure all of that out later—now is the time for celebrating," said my mom. "I wish I could be there with you. I love you all."

"I love you, mom," I said, fighting tears of joy.

I handed Bram his phone and then beckoned to everyone to come close—Nerida, Bram, Rick, Argo, Squeak, Gibber, and all the Play Things and ZETHs on the stage. "Bring it in, guys," I said.

We embraced each other in a big, victorious group hug of love and teamwork.

I swelled with pride, knowing that no matter how bad things got, no matter how troubled the seas became, I would never, ever, have to handle it alone.

"Good work, princess," said Nerida with a wink.

And I wasn't even mad.

ACKNOWLEDGMENTS

Many thanks to Andrea Reuter, Reneé Yama, Jenny Bowman, and Derek Sullivan for your storytelling, creative, and editorial acumen. Your contributions have deeply enhanced this book. Thank you to Hazy Dell Press for your belief in this book from the jump. Thank you to Ellie for your constant support. And thank you to all the readers—without you, this story would be nothing but a sea of meaningless words, words, words.

Head to **hazydellpress.com** for Hazy Dell Press titles for all ages, including *Hazy Fables #1: Hobgoblin and the Seven Stinkers of Rancidia.*

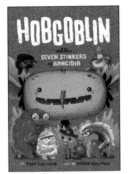

**Middle-Grade Books
Ages 8-12**

**Picture Books
Ages 5-12**

**Board Books
Ages 1-7**

**Flap Books
Ages 0-4**

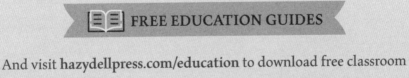

📖 **FREE EDUCATION GUIDES**

And visit **hazydellpress.com/education** to download free classroom education guides for *Zombie, Or Not to Be*, including a guide to all the Shakespeare references and allusions in the book.